AVERY TAYLOR

Whispers at Willowmere Farm

Millie Wright Mystery #1

For Lexington, Kentucky, and all the horses I've been lucky enough to meet and care for here. This book would have been impossible without you.

Contents

Chapter 1

Millie Wright sat cross legged in the grass, breathing in the damp, earthy air. The backyard of the house where she was staying overlooked acres of fields, grazing Thoroughbreds dotting the land. The scene was so picturesque, so serene, that she wished she could freeze the moment in time.

Her stomach churned with nerves, she had yet to meet her roommate for the next few months, a girl named Jessica Howell. Millie had tried to look her up on the internet, only finding out that she was a redhead in her early thirties.

She stood, brushing bits of grass and dirt off her denim jeans. She figured she should unpack, maybe take a walk around the farm. Of course, she had no idea where anything was, and got the impression that it was the sort of place where you could get lost if you didn't know where you were headed. Narrow roads surrounded endless fenced pastures, creating an infinite maze. Perhaps unpacking would be best, at least until her roommate showed up. That is, assuming she was a bit more helpful than the foreman who had gotten her from the airport.

Sloane was a dark haired woman who was uninterested in making conversation on the brief ride to the cottage. "The

Jennings' are unavailable, so they sent me to pick you up," she flatly explained from the driver's seat of a white truck, *Willowmere Farm* written on the door. "I don't know when they'll be back."

"Oh," Millie replied, trying to hide her disappointment . "I didn't realize they were out of town."

"They're not," she clarified. "Mr. Jennings got himself trampled by a horse last night. Kelly is with him at the trauma center in Louisville."

Millie was taken aback. "Oh my gosh, is he okay?"

"Define 'okay'. Last I heard, he's conscious and breathing. No clue the extent of his injuries, but I'd assume they're not great."

Millie furrowed her eyebrows. "What happened?" she inquired. "You said he was trampled?"

"Yup. Stewart—he's the yearling manager—said some year-ling colts got loose. Night watch called after midnight to get help. From there, I guess it's not hard to figure out what happened. Pitch black out, loose colts on a farm full of mares. One plus one equals two, you know?"

"How did they get loose?"

"Gate was left open. Of course, no one is taking responsibility for it," she rolled her eyes.

The rest of the car ride passed in silence, Millie feeling an impending sense of doom despite her original excitement. She felt very small in the cloth covered passenger seat, the growing desire to shrink herself curling up from deep inside her.

The interior of the truck was covered with dust and old crumbs, the backseat piled high with broken halters and crumpled potato chip bags. *Disgusting.* The view from the window changed from asphalt and freeway to narrow farm roads, green fields pressing in from both sides. If she hadn't been so nervous, Millie would have been in awe of the seemingly endless expanse of green grass and bur oaks.

Sloane slowed and turned into a gated driveway, punching in a code before rolling forward. "5343 is the code," she informed Millie, staring straight ahead. "Not sure how much you'll need it though, seeing as you didn't bring a car."

Millie bit her tongue and took in the scenery. Rolling hills in every direction, a barn standing proudly on top of a hill. Mares and foals wandered in distant fields, a rippling pond catching the light. The place looked more like a golf course than a horse farm.

When they reached a four way stop, Sloane turned the car left. They passed some more barns, and made enough turns to completely disorient Millie, before pulling up to a modest brown cottage.

"This is where you'll be staying," Sloane informed her, fiddling with a key ring, "You'll be living with Jessica, she can fill you in on house rules. I've got your house key here for you," she said, holding out an old brass key.

Millie hopped out, grabbing her purse and luggage. She was left standing alone in the driveway before she could even utter 'Thank you'.

"Hey! You must be Millie!" a tall, red haired girl called out from the doorway.

Millie stood up and extended her hand. "Yes, that's me."

"I'm Jessica, you'll be staying here with me for the summer. I'd be happy to give you a tour of the place, if you'd like? Normally the Jennings' like to show new hires around themselves, but since they're not here, Sloane asked me to give you the lay of the land."

"Yes, I'd love that," Millie replied, silently relieved that her roommate was showing signs of an actual personality. "Just let me know when you want to go."

Jessica shrugged, gesturing to her casual outfit. "I just got off work, so we can go now if you want?"

Millie threw her sneakers on, and together the two girls walked between two fields and up a hill to the nearest barn. "We'll grab the golf cart from the foaling barn to explore the rest of the property," Jessica explained. "The farm is too large for us to check out everything on foot, unless we want to be out here all night."

"Oh wow," Millie breathed out as she looked up at the arched doorways of the ornate wooden barn. Walking into the stable, she heard the gentle sounds of mares munching on hay. Peeking into the first stall, she saw a tall chestnut mare standing over a tiny bay foal laying at her hooves.

The aisle was immaculately clean, with gleaming brass name-plates on each stall and hardly a speck of dust anywhere. "This place looks cleaner than my room back home," Millie laughed.

"I know! All of the foaling mares stay up here. The Jennings' have very high standards, so everything is well kept, but this barn especially. We keep it so clean because all the foals up here are newborns, and their immune systems aren't fully developed yet. At the end of every day, the floor, doors, and walls get sprayed down with a disinfectant mixture to help prevent any sickness from spreading around."

Millie nodded in understanding. "How many foals do you have every year?"

"Roughly forty to fifty, born between January and May. We only have fourteen mares left to foal out this year. I think Nighty Night will go next," Jessica said, pointing to a dark bay mare across the aisle. The mare shifted uncomfortably as they looked in, her large, distended stomach looking as if it was about pop. "How will you know when she's having it?" Millie asked curiously.

"The farm is staffed 24/7, so there's always someone around. The expectant mares are only alone when night watch has to run out to check on the other horses here. And even then, there are cameras in each foaling stall that we can all watch at any time. After her water breaks, whoever is on watch will call the Jennings'. Every year though, it seems there's always one that foals without us noticing, usually out in the field."

"Have you heard any updates on Mr. Jennings?" Millie asked anxiously, "Sloane said he was hurt?"

Jessica's subtle frown lines deepened. "I haven't heard much, no. Stewart handled the vet this morning and organized the schedule today, so I think he's in charge until they come back."

Jessica led her to a spacious double size stall, the walls banked high with fluffy bedding. "This is the foaling stall. If one of the mares is getting ready to foal, do your best to get her in here. The larger stall is much safer for everyone, and we bed it extra deep for the newborns."

They continued their walk down the aisle, peeking in each stall before pausing at a black mare with a glossy coat. The mare was wide eyed and alert, pawing the ground and snorting every so often. "Is someone supposed to be up here watching them?" Millie asked in concern. She hadn't worked around many pregnant mares, but she was a skilled horsewoman from spending summers at her aunt's Hunter/Jumper stable in New Hampshire. To Millie, the mare looked distressed enough to warrant a close eye on her.

Jessica nodded. "Chloe is on the 4—7 shift tonight. She should be back soon, she's probably just checking the rest of the farm right now. I'll text her about this mare, but I'm not worried. She has a ways to go."

Millie looked at the mare's enormous stomach and busy hooves, and glanced at Jessica in disbelief.

Jessica laughed. "You'll get used to this. This is Venus Rising, a maiden mare—that's what we call a mare who has never had a baby. She's not quite sure what her body is doing, it makes them a little nervous the first time. The old girls, they know what's up and don't get so worried about it," she explained, gesturing to a gray flecked chestnut across the aisle. The mare's eyes were heavy, her head positioned against a stall wall with her hind leg resting in the deep straw. "Candy Queen has had nine or ten foals I think, this will be her last before she gets retired. You see how relaxed she is? I'd bet you anything that she goes before that silly maiden."

Millie found this hard to believe, but didn't want to question Jessica too much, so followed silently as she walked over to a beat up golf cart. A half full bag of grain and a collection of feed buckets rattled around the passenger seat. "Just throw all that in the aisle," Jessica advised.

"Oh shoot," Jessica muttered under her breath. 'Do you have your house key on you?"

"Yes?" Millie replied, unsure of where the conversation was going.

"Oh good, can you give it to me? The key isn't in the ignition, and I don't feel like tracking it down right now. Sloane's been so paranoid about farm equipment disappearing around Lexington, she probably took it."

"And my house key will help you how?" Millie asked, disbelieving.

"These older golf carts will take most any type of key," Jessica confided, pointing her finger at Millie. "But don't you ever use that to steal one, understand?"

Sure enough, the key turned over smoothly, and Jessica drove Millie around the entire farm. Millie wasn't entirely sure she was going to be able to remember all of the identical barns the following day, but appreciated Jessica's never ending commentary. As they watched yearlings play in the soft glow of the setting sun, Millie squinted her eyes and looked in the distance. "What's that out there?" she asked, nodding towards a stone enclosure sitting atop a hill.

"That's the old farm graveyard. Do you want to go take a look?"

She shrugged, feigning indifference though she was dying to investigate. "Sure."

The stone wall surrounding the graveyard was about waist high. Jessica carefully positioned the golf cart next to it so they could climb over easily. Millie strolled towards the closest grave marker, obscured with moss and earth. Large and ornate, it was difficult to make out the crumbling words.

Jessica crouched down next to her and brushed off the letters with the back of her hand. *—1854* was the only script legible. "I think most of these graves belong to the Lockhurst family, though I don't know much about who they were. Those ones over there," she said, pointing to a collection of tiny gravestones, only about a foot tall, "They're all for children."

Millie stood and walked over to them. *Tobias Lockhurst 1826—1835*, a crumbling stone read. Many of the small stones were for babies, she noted somberly.

A patch of pink lilies grew in each corner of the yard. "Who maintains the graveyard?" she asked. Though the gravestones were in poor condition, it was clear someone had cared for the area. The grass was freshly cut, the stone wall appeared as if it had been stacked that week instead of more than a century ago, and someone had gone to the trouble of planting flowers.

Jessica shrugged. "I'm not really sure. Maintenance, probably. I've never seen anyone out here before." her eyes glanced up at the moon peeking out from behind the clouds. "We should probably head back to the house and feed you dinner before it gets too late."

Millie agreed, carefully climbing the wall to get out. Driving away, she couldn't help but glance back, the hairs on the back of her neck standing.

Chapter 2

"Y ou ready for your first day?!" Jessica asked with a smile as they walked out to her car.

Millie nodded silently, her teeth chattering. The morning had dawned cool and bright, a thick layer of fog giving the farm an ethereal look. She was from Vermont, used to cold winters, but somehow didn't feel prepared to face the brisk spring air. "I thought Kentucky was warm," she sputtered out, diving to turn on her seat heater.

Jessica cackled. "Kentucky in spring is a fickle beast. You just wait, it'll be 90 degrees by afternoon, and then it will snow tomorrow!"

Millie shook her head. "It better not, I didn't leave New England just so I could get snowed in on a horse farm!"

Jessica hurriedly answered her phone as it started ringing. "Uh huh," she muttered, "Yeah, I've got her here with me. I'll bring her up now."

The churning of nerves that had nearly overtaken her the day before, threatened again. She gnawed on the inside of her cheek, wondering what the day ahead would bring.

Jessica turned to her with a tight smile. "That was Stewart. He wants you to start at the foaling barn with Sloane. I'll drop you there, then I'll head up to the Maiden Mare Barn. You can call me if you need anything, okay?"

Millie had been hoping that she just got off on the wrong foot with Sloane, but the note of sympathy in Jessica's voice worried her. "Great, thank you," she told Jessica as she hopped out, and then marched forward into the foaling barn with butterflies in her stomach. Walking down the aisle, she tried to memorize each mare's face. It seemed so overwhelming, needing to familiarize yourself with twenty new horses, but Millie knew she'd know them all before long.

At the end of the aisle, she saw Sloane, crouched down with her cell phone flashlight shining underneath a mare's stomach. Sloane briefly turned to her. "Oh. hi," she muttered.

"What are you doing?" Millie inquired.

"Checking this mare's udder," she replied bluntly, hesitating before continuing on. "As they get closer to foaling, their udder will get larger and develop a yellowish serum on the end of their teats, called wax. Quotation here just developed wax this morning. Want to look?"

Millie nodded with enthusiasm and crouched down. "I see why it's called wax, it looks just like drippings from a wax candle,"

Sloane nodded her head. "We can test her milk later to find out more, but this tells us that she's getting pretty close to having her foal."

They exited the stall and grabbed lead shanks to begin leading the mares out to their respective pastures. It took both of them to lead the mare and foal pairs, with Millie leading the mare and Sloane guiding the foal. "We'll get you handling the foals soon here, once you've watched me with them a little. They're awfully cute and cuddly, but it's easy to forget they're just tiny athletes with no manners. They will take any chance to step on your feet and jump on you," she nodded, observing Sloane's personality change with fascination. With the foals, she was enthusiastic and kind, quick to laugh and offer a gentle correction when needed.

Before long, they were left with an empty barn that needed to be mucked out. "I'll grab the tractor from outside. Go ahead and grab us pitchforks and rakes, they're in the last stall on the right." Sloane said before striding outside.

With tools in hand, Millie walked to the first stall on the left and began sorting through the wet straw and manure. The straw bedding, ideal for newborn foals, was heavier and harder to clean than the shavings Millie was used to, but she adjusted quickly. Absorbed in her task, she didn't stop to wonder what was taking Sloane so long.

Two stalls later, she heard a scream from outside!

Millie dropped her pitchfork and sprinted out the barn doors, looking around for Sloane. There was a loud buzzing sound in the air. The older girl was shaking, her face white with shock. "What happened?!" Millie asked urgently.

"I—I was looking for the tractor keys," she sniffled, "They're always left in the ignition, but they weren't there. So I started looking for them. I was feeling around for them on the floor, and I guess I must have disturbed a hornets nest? I was checking right behind the brake pedal, and," she held up her swollen hand.

"Are you allergic?" Millie knew this could be a dangerous situation if Sloane had a reaction to the wasps venom.

"No, but, I must have been stung ten or fifteen times,"

Millie examined Sloane's hand closely, trying to remember everything she had learned from a first aid course she had attended. "Let's ice it right now, and try to find someone to take you to urgent care. Just in case."

With Sloane sitting in the tack room, icing her hand and whimpering in pain, Millie stepped outside. Unsure of what to do, she dialed Jessica's phone number, praying she would answer.

Words spilled out of Millie after Jessica picked up the phone. Once she finished explaining what had happened, there was a moment of silence.

"Wow. Oh my gosh. Um, let me call Stewart. If he's not on the farm, I'll come up and take her somewhere." They quickly finished their conversation and hung up. Millie gnawed on her bottom lip, her mind spinning with thought. *What a strange place for a hornets nest.*

She ducked into the feed room to grab a bucket, and filled it with water and soap from underneath the sink. Her father had taught her this trick years before to eliminate minor wasp and hornet problems—a bucket of soapy water would kill them almost instantly. Discreetly peeking through the tack room window to make sure Sloane wasn't succumbing to anaphylactic shock, Millie strode out towards the tractor with caution. She lifted her bucket high and tossed the water onto the tractor floor, jumping back nervously.

Waiting a moment to be sure she had taken care of the nest, her eyes quickly swept the interior. The tractor keys laid behind the clutch pedal, right next to the nest. She wasn't sure what else she was looking for but didn't see anything obviously amiss. She began to turn away at the sound of a truck pulling up the barn's drive, but something caught her eye—a men's wrist watch. Millie grabbed it and stuck it in her pocket before looking back to make sure no one had seen her.

Back at the barn, a tall, pale man had just arrived and was examining Sloane's hand. He looked up at Millie and offered his hand. "I'm Stewart, the yearling foreman. You must be Millie? I'm sorry we're not meeting under better circumstances."

Millie shook his hand and smiled tightly. "Yes, a rather exciting first day, I'd say."

Stewart quickly explained that he was taking Sloane to the hospital. "It's swelled to twice its normal size, better safe than sorry," he sighed, the creases in his forehead deepening. "I'm sending the maintenance crew over to check the tractor for any more hidden nests. In the meantime, you can start working on cleaning the barn—dumping the water buckets, mucking the stalls into the aisle, and someone will be up to help in a little while. Just make sure to check the pregnant mares every fifteen minutes or so, you never know when one will try to foal unexpectedly."

Stewart and Sloane drove off and it took no time at all for Millie to settle into the familiar rhythm of barn chores. She made fast work of it, humming along to the radio as she went. After every stall, she ran out to the pregnant mares field to do a headcount before starting on the next. Before Millie knew it, all the water buckets had been dumped and the dirty bedding from the stalls was mucked into the aisle, ready to be thrown up into a muck wagon once a tractor was available.

Just then, Millie heard the roar of a tractor pulling up the drive towards the barn. "Perfect timing!" Millie shouted above the loud engine, spotting Jessica in the driver's seat.

Jessica grinned, shutting the engine off. "I came to help, but it looks like you got things under control here," she said, nodding to the neat piles of muck left in the aisle. Together the two girls lifted the manure into the muck wagon, added hay and straw bedding to the stalls, and swept the aisle clean.

Jessica nodded in satisfaction at the barn aisle before glancing down to check her watch. "The mornings here go pretty fast, don't they?! It's already lunch time. Let's take the golf cart back to the house and I'll make us some food."

Millie glanced nervously towards the mare pasture. "Is it okay to leave the mares alone? Stewart told me to check them every fifteen minutes."

Jessica kept walking, waving a hand flippantly. "We rotate who watches them over lunch. One of the maintenance guys is doing it today. Terry, I think."

Across the scuffed wooden table Jessica looked at Millie appraisingly. "We haven't really gotten a chance to talk to each other, have we? We were so busy looking at the farm last night, I don't think I even asked where you're from. Tell me a little about yourself."

Millie took a large bite of her taco so she would have time to think of an appropriate answer while she chewed. There were few things she hated more than being put on the spot. "I'm not very interesting," she explained apologetically. "Born and raised in Vermont. My aunt has a riding stable over the New Hampshire border, that's where I learned most of what I know about horses. I graduated high school a semester early, want to go to vet school, and hate mayonnaise. Not much else to me."

"You must have been a good student," she smirked, Millie's eye twitching at the fleck of cheese dangling from the corner of Jessica's mouth. "What do your parents do?"

"They own a gift shop and run it together. Usually, I mean. Dad is hiking the Appalachian trail this summer, so Mom will run it herself."

Jessica looked at Millie as if she had grown another head. "I'm going to need more details than that, girl," shaking her head in disbelief. "What kind of gift shop? And how does your mother feel about her husband running off to go on a nature walk?"

She's completely livid and it's very possible she'll never let Dad back in the house, Millie thought to herself, taking a drink from her cold water glass to stall. "It's a gift shop, they sell, you know, gift shop stuff. Knick knacks, sweatshirts, lots of handmade Vermont sweaters and earrings. The tourists go crazy for anything 'authentic Vermont', even if the yarn came from China." she paused for a moment, folding over the corner of her napkin. "My Mom would probably prefer I was there to run the shop with her. Dad has always been a real outdoors man, he's wanted to do the Appalachian trail for a long time. It was no surprise to her."

Jessica shrugged. "You got a boyfriend back home then?"

"No!" Millie snapped. "I would've never had time, between school, working the shop, helping my aunt."

"Whatever you say," Jessica teased, scraping her chair back against the floor. "We should get going. I'll leave you at the Foaling Barn again while I head go help Chloe turn out the retired mares. All that's left for you to do is make the medicine and supplements for the mares, put feed in the stalls, and fill the water buckets. If you have time, spray the aisle with the disinfectant that's in the supply room. And make sure you check the whiteboard to see which horse gets what, they all get something a bit different. Chloe and I will come back in a few hours to help you bring the mares in."

As Millie carefully measured out scoops of feed and teaspoons of Chinese herbs, she found her mind wandering back to the morning's events. How was it possible that a mature wasps nest had developed so quickly, in a tractor that was used daily? Was it possible it had been planted? But why?

Her chain of thought was interrupted by the sound of a truck pulling up to the front doors of the barn. She stepped out of the feed room, and almost ran into a lanky young man, barely older than her, with messy brown hair. "Hey," he smiled. "Are you the new girl? I'm Joe, I work in maintenance usually."

Joe was soft spoken and had an ease about him that made her want to like him. "I'm Millie," she offered. "I'm guessing you came up to take a look at the tractor?".

Joe held up a can of wasp spray. "You got it. Did you happen to see where they were coming from?"

"I actually think I might have killed them," she admitted sheepishly. "I threw a bucket of soapy water on the nest behind the clutch, so I could take a quick look inside."

He raised his eyebrows. "That was brave of you. Can I ask what was so important in there that you wanted to risk getting attacked by wasps?"

Millie shook her head. "I mean, I don't want to sound paranoid. But isn't that kind of weird? For a wasp's nest to develop overnight, when they apparently use that tractor every day?"

Joe shrugged. "Hornets and yellow jackets can be pretty quick about it. Usually late summer though, not spring," he frowned, looking thoughtful. "If you're implying they were, I don't know, planted or something? I'm not sure that's even possible."

Millie backpedaled. "No, of course not, I just was... curious, that's all. I'm sorry I didn't wait for you to come check it out before I did that."

They walked towards the tractor, their strides matching. "I

wouldn't have thought you were crazy if you said yes, for the record."

Millie wasn't sure how to reply, so she remained silent as Joe swung open the tractor door and climbed up to look around. "Well Millie, I think you took care of them all, I don't see any other nests. You should be fine using it tomorrow." He kicked the soggy, empty nest out with the toe of his boot. "Just do me a favor and don't go messing with any more wasps nests?"

"Of course," she agreed, her mind buzzing with questions.

Jessica introduced Chloe as "The town crier of Willowmere," a title that Millie thought was fitting.

Millie laughed good-naturedly as the bubbly blonde stepped forward. "That's me," Chloe grinned, an assessing glint in her eye. "Don't try to get anything past me, because I will find out!"

Millie couldn't tell if the older girl was kidding or not, but chose to smile as if she was. "I'll remember that! Since you're plugged into everyone here, tell me about my new co-workers."

Chloe frowned. "There's not many of us right now. You, me, Jessica, and Sloane on the mares. Just Eduardo and Stewart caring for the yearlings, and Joe is filling in as maintenance manager until they find someone else. There's two part time guys that help him, but I hardly ever see them."

"Do they usually keep more staff?" Millie inquired. "It doesn't seem like a lot of people to care for a herd this size."

Jessica nodded grimly. "Once we finish foaling, we'll have over one hundred horses."

"This is a bit of a skeleton crew, a lot of people have left recently," Chloe admitted. "I'm not sure how unique that is though. Farm jobs tend to be high turnover. Long hours, low pay, and everyone is hiring, so if you don't like something you can just go find another job down the street."

"It comes in waves too," Jessica offered. "You might get two or three friends that come to work together, and when one leaves, they all go. Luckily there's only a month or so left of the foaling season."

"The Jennings' better find some people fast, before yearling prep starts," Chloe quipped.

"I'm sure they'll figure it out," Millie offered.

One by one, the girls brought in the pregnant mares for the night. Millie found it so satisfying to put each mare in their own deeply bedded stall with freshly scrubbed buckets, as if she was tucking them in for the night.

They were about to start picking out each mare's hooves, filled with muck and stones from their day outside, when a navy truck pulled up to the barn. Stewart rolled the window down and rubbed his face. *He looks exhausted*, Millie thought to herself, observing the dark circles under his eyes and slumped posture.

"I just spoke with Sloane. She's doing okay, but they're keeping her for observation tonight and the doctors advised her to take it easy for the rest of the week. With the Jennings' still gone, that means night watch and I are the only ones around if any mares foal tonight. Would you and Jessica mind being on call in case anything happens?"

Millie nodded excitedly. She had a special interest in foaling since seeing a foal born at her aunt's farm as a child. She knew that mares usually liked to give birth in the middle of the night, but in Millie's opinion, it was well worth losing sleep over.

Jessica laughed at Millie's enthusiasm. "Sure, why wouldn't I volunteer to hang out in a barn at two in the morning?! Of course we'll help, Stewart."

Stewart let out a sigh. "Thanks girls. I hate to ask, but we're shorthanded already, only having one night watchman. And as you know, foaling isn't my usual forte. Having some extra sets of hands on deck might be a good idea."

Jessica nodded. "Of course. Nighty Night is waxed pretty heavily and wasn't very interested in her grain. She might foal tonight."

Stewart sighed in disappointment. "Honestly, I was hoping they would all just hold off until the Jennings' are back. There's a reason I stopped dealing with foaling mares, and it wasn't because I was getting too much sleep."

Chapter 3

Millie was in her pajamas, fluffing her pillow for the night when her phone rang. "Hello?"

"Millie, it's Stewart. Night watch just called and said Nighty Night is getting ready to have her foal. She just went down and is sweating heavily. Can you get Jessica and meet me at the foaling barn?"

"Yes, we'll be there as soon as we can. See you there," she responded, yanking jeans and socks out of her suitcase.

She threw open the door to the back porch, Jessica jumping in surprise "Nighty Night is foaling!" she declared.

Jessica didn't need further prompting. They ran to her jeep and began the short drive to the foaling barn in tense silence. Upon arriving, Jessica pulled up to the front doors of the barn and yanked the keys out of the ignition. Millie quickly strode into the dim barn aisle, following the sounds of a mare groaning and muffled voices. Turning the corner, she was greeted by the sight of the mare nuzzling her still wet newborn. The foal was laying down, stretching their nose out towards their mother. "Wow, she must have gone fast!" Millie remarked. "Is it a boy or a girl?"

It's a colt, which is what we call baby boys around here,"

Stewart explained. "Nighty Night is like this every year, she'll be quiet as a mouse, and next thing you know she'll be laying down having her baby."

Millie noticed a petite woman standing over the foal, holding a towel covered in blood and horsehair. "Is that the night watchman?" she muttered to Jessica.

Jessica nodded. "Connie, this is our newest intern, Millie. She's here to learn more about how a breeding farm works. I imagine you'll be seeing a lot of each other."

The dark haired woman gave a curt nod. "Well Millie, I hope you like late nights, because that's about the only time anything ever happens around here."

"Oh look!" Millie exclaimed. "He's trying to get up!" The foal stretched his front legs out, struggling for traction so he could pull himself up.

Connie stepped forward and began to help arrange the foal's front legs, uncrossing them and bringing them out in front of his body. She reached to help support his hind end as he attempted to stand for the first time. Just as the foal was trying to pull himself up, the lights flickered once, and then shut off entirely, leaving them in the pitch black!

Millie froze and waited for her eyes to adjust to the darkness. A half moon shone through a stall window across the aisle, providing minimal light. It was just enough for Millie to get her bearings. "Is everyone okay?" she asked.

"Yes, but what happened?!" Jessica asked.

"It's a perfectly clear night," Stewart said, sounding puzzled.

"Maybe something doesn't want us here," Connie replied shortly.

Millie was taken aback. "What do you mean, Connie?"

"Nothing, nothing at all." Connie scoffed.

Before Millie could question her further, the foal resumed his attempts to stand. Flailing like a wet fish, they cringed as he tumbled sideways.

Stewart spoke up. "Okay, I want someone to come with me down to maintenance, and have two people stay back here and watch the foal. Millie, come with me?"

Millie cautiously stepped away from the stall door she was leaning against and stretched her arms out to feel around her. "If nothing else, maybe we can grab flashlights at the maintenance building?"

"Hopefully this is just a temporary power outage,"

The two made their way out of the barn, Millie halting immediately outside the doors. "Stewart, look over there. The yearlings have their lights on!"

"There shouldn't be anyone at yearlings," Stewart replied, sounding puzzled. "We better go down there to check it out."

Stewart drove the truck straight to the yearling barn. With the young horses all turned out for the night, the barn was still and quiet. "Hello?" Millie called out, peering through the open stall doors. "Is anyone here?"

Her only answer was a mouse scampering through the straw. Millie and Stewart walked down the aisle, each taking a side, before finally meeting at the tack room. "I don't know Millie," Stewart said, "Maybe Connie just forgot to turn the lights out last time she did rounds. I'm not sure why she would have been in here, but maybe she was looking for something. We need to hurry over to maintenance and then get back to the new foal."

Millie was quiet as they drove, her mind heavy with thought.

At the maintenance building, she walked behind Stewart, her cell phone flashlight illuminating the concrete block building.

Stewart fussed with a large key ring by the garage entrance, before finding a brass one that unlocked the door. "I think the power supply is on the back wall somewhere," he muttered to himself.

Meanwhile, Millie zeroed in on a framed map hung on the wall straight ahead. Barns, pastures, and houses were carefully drawn and labeled on the map. Millie traced her finger down the intersecting roads, trying to find her house. *This must be an old map*, she figured, noting the lack of smaller paddocks and nonexistent staff housing. Squinting her eyes to look closer at the barns, she noticed a small extension off of the feed room in the Yearling barn.

"Does the Yearling barn have an extra stall or office next to the feed room?" She shouted to Stewart in the next room over.

She heard metal clanking and footsteps, and Stewart appeared in the doorway, carrying four flashlights. "What?" he asked, sounding confused.

"The map." Millie pointed her cell phone at the Yearling barn on the map. "It shows an extension on one side."

"Oh, that," Stewart replied distractedly. "That's just a copy of the original farm map, from when the farm was first built about a hundred years ago. So much has changed, the old well is gone, the old assistant's cottage burned down thirty years ago… maybe that was extra storage or something, but it's long gone now."

Following him through the doorway, she breathed in the scent of old rubber and oil. Along the back wall was a series of switches and breakers, each set labeled for a different barn or building. Stewart muttered under his breath, searching for the foaling barn label.

Millie knew when he found it, because his muttering ceased,

and he immediately stilled.

"What on earth…"Stewart said softly.

Millie peeked over his shoulder. "What's wrong?" she asked.

Stewart shook his head. "You see these switches? Someone went through and turned them off. If the breaker had flipped for some reason, the switch would be right in the middle."

"Weird," Millie replied, noncommittally. "Why would someone do that?"

"I haven't the faintest idea. At least it's an easy fix," he offered wryly, flipping each switch in the row.

Now brightly lit, Stewart and Millie returned to the Foaling barn. Connie and Jessica were watching the new colt with rapt attention. Dried off, his coat was a handsome copper chestnut. With long spindly legs, he was just strong enough to hold his body up as he took his first steps in the deep straw. Millie noticed that while Jessica looked relaxed, Connie was frowning, her eyes hollow.

"Get everything fixed?" Jessica asked curiously.

Stewart nodded and began to explain how the breaker switches had been flipped off. Connie shook her head with disdain, grabbing the foaling kit and marching off to the tack room. Wordlessly, Millie grabbed an unused package of latex gloves and followed after Connie. "Where would you like me to put these?" Millie asked.

"Just set them somewhere and I'll take care of it," Connie snapped back.

Millie set the box on the counter, hanging back awkwardly in hopes Connie would strike up a conversation. The older woman whirled around the room with fervent purpose, throwing out wads of used gloves, carefully measuring blue liquid into a spray bottle, and wiping out the red plastic grooming tote containing everything. "Do you mind showing me how you put together a foaling kit?" Millie asked.

Connie grimaced. "We have a list somewhere, but sure, you can watch. Most important thing here is a clean, sharp pair of scissors. Next, you'll want a container of chlorhexidine—that's this blue stuff in the spray bottle here—or iodine for disinfecting the umbilical stump. You also want something to clamp off the end of that if you have a bleeder.

"Mares should get their tails wrapped up before they break water so you're not fighting with hair, that's what the vet wrap is for. You should always have clean towels to dry off the foal, and an enema to help it pass meconium. Oh, and Banamine for the mare, to help with the pain immediately after foaling. Standard baling twine off a bale of hay is never a bad idea either, you never know when you'll need it. Hospital gowns, shoulder length plastic sleeves, and nitrile gloves, so you hopefully don't have to smell like blood and amniotic fluid the rest of the day," she offered a thin smile. "We also have an oxygen tank with us for every foaling. We almost never use it, but that's the sort of thing you can't be hunting down when you need it—it can be the difference between a live foal and a dead foal. Got all that?"

Millie gulped, nodding solemnly. She felt confident that she would never be able to remember everything. "How long have you been doing this?" she asked in a timid voice.

Connie laughed. "Longer than you've been alive, probably. It's not rocket science, but you do need to pay attention. There's an endless list of things that can go wrong. I sometimes think the average horse person has no clue how treacherous bringing them into the world can be."

Millie nodded in understanding. "I've been around horses

most of my life, and I've only seen one mare foal. Weird to think I've been riding all these years, but had no clue how to put together a foaling kit."

Connie seemed more relaxed now, smiling warmly. "That's normal though. Kentucky will get you up to speed on horse midwifery before you know it. You'll catch on quick."

Millie hesitated, unsure of her next move. "Kind of weird tonight with the lights, eh?" she offered.

A dark cloud passed over Connie's face. "I'm not sure 'weird' is the word I would use."

"What do you mean?"

"Stuff like that has been happening for ages. You'll see for yourself. Folks think it's funny to joke about ghosts, but I'm tellin' you, something on this farm isn't happy."

"Ghosts?" she asked with skepticism. "Have you ever seen one?"

Connie glanced around, searching the room for something only she could see. She began to speak, just as Jessica walked into the tack room. "Are you about ready to head home, Millie?" Jessica asked obliviously, as Connie slunk out of the room.

"Yeah, sure," Millie sighed, hiding her disappointment.

Chapter 4

The morning air was crisp as an apple, the thick fog lending an autumn feel to the day. Sitting in the passenger seat of Jessica's jeep, Millie was tired from the excitement of the night, but was becoming energized at the prospect of a new day. The watch she found yesterday weighed heavily in the pocket of her jeans. She quietly hoped to hear more gossip about the farm, suspecting what Connie had let slip was only the tip of the iceberg.

"I doubt Sloane will be back today, so I think we'll all end up working together again. Stewart texted me and said to leave you at the Foaling barn to do morning medication, then start turning out the mares. Leave Nighty Night and her colt inside, the vet will be by this morning to check them out anyways. I'll meet up with Chloe to help her feed the mares and older foals outside this morning, then we'll come back to help you muck out. That okay with you?"

"Yep, sounds good," Millie agreed, biting back a wave of nervousness. She felt unprepared to work alone. What if one of the mares started to foal and she didn't notice? *I'm just going to have to be extra diligent*, she told herself grimly.

Jessica dropped off Millie with a parting wave. Breathing in the scent of wet straw, she picked her first task, checking in with all the pregnant mares. Trying to remember everything she had read in *Blessed are the Broodmares*, one by one she visited with each mare. First, she assessed their general demeanor, then peeked under their belly to see if they had waxed or were dripping milk. Running a careful hand over their hindquarters, she checked to see if the muscles and ligaments surrounding their tail head had relaxed in preparation of foaling. As she stood up and patted the neck of Dorothy B, a small bay mare who was just starting to wax, she squinted at something in the straw.

Frowning, Millie felt around for the glittering object before grasping it. "A lighter?" she muttered under her breath. *Why would that be here in the stable?* She held it up to the light, flipping it over for examination. It looked old, with ornate etching in the metal, *J L D* engraved on the backside. Shrugging, Millie slipped it into her pocket—she'd try to track down its owner later.

Millie released the last mare into the large front pasture, watching as the group of them cantered off into the fog. She chewed on the inside of her cheek, puzzling over the watch and the lighter. Should she tell anyone? After all, she had no idea who they belonged to, or if they even had nefarious intent. Of course, both could have been a complete accident, a faulty clasp on the watch, a hole in the pocket of someone who smokes.

Maybe it would be best to at least keep the lighter quiet, she thought to herself. Even if it was an accident, Millie had a deep rooted fear of barn fires. Her Grandfather's voice echoed in her head, reminding her of how easily a barn could ignite, with their infinite supply of dust, cobwebs, straw, and hay.

She made quick work of cleaning stalls, and had mucked

almost half the barn into the aisle by the time Chloe and Jessica arrived with the tractor and muck wagon. Together, the girls breezed through the rest of chores. Millie thought they worked well together as a group—Chloe being the most detail oriented, Millie the fastest, and Jessica keeping them all entertained with conversation and music as they completed their duties.

They had just finished filling water buckets when Stewart's truck pulled into the barn.

Jessica went up to talk to him, Millie and Chloe hanging back to portion out the mare's afternoon medicine. Their discussion became animated, with Jessica shaking her head and Stewart looking exasperated.

After several minutes, Stewart looked at Millie and motioned her over. "Millie, I know you just started, but Jessica says you've got the lay of the land already. Would you be willing to do the night watch shift for us this week?"

Millie was taken aback. "Night watch? I wouldn't even know what to do."

"It's not hard," Jessica said. "Really it's just filling water buckets, and checking on the foaling mares. Making sure no one is sick or actively giving birth. If the mares are quiet, you'll drive the maintenance truck out to check on the older foals, yearlings, maiden and retired mares once or twice."

Stewart nodded. "Yes, and if anyone starts to foal, or you have any questions you can always call me. I'm on call until whenever the Jennings' get back."

Millie swallowed nervously. "I'll do it," she agreed. "I'm a little nervous that I'll miss something, but I'll give it a try, sure."

Stewart looked relieved. "Great, great," he said. "I'm going to send you back home now to rest. I'll have Jessica bring you back here at 7 o'clock tonight, and she'll do your first round with you to make sure you've got the hang of it."

An odd feeling crawled up Millie's spine. "Stewart, why do you need me to cover night watch? Is Connie sick?"

Stewart and Jessica shared an uncomfortable glance. "Well," he began. "I got a phone call at 3:30 this morning. From Connie. She, erm, quit on the spot."

"What? Why?!" Millie asked in shock.

Jessica rolled her eyes. "Apparently the radio was turning itself off and on last night. And something about bucket clips snapping and unsnapping themselves... Connie said it started shortly after we left. The radio is probably just faulty, and I bet she imagined the clips, but I suppose she was pretty spooked."

Millie raised an eyebrow. "Has this ever happened before?"

Stewart gave a halfhearted laugh. "I mean, there have always been rumors about this farm. It's old, there's a graveyard, people's imaginations sometimes get away from them. But no, this is not a common occurrence. I'm willing to bet Connie was just too tired. She's been working overtime since January, she may feel differently about what she experienced in a few days."

"Right," Millie replied, feeling skeptical. She paused, looking between the two of them, "Before I forget, do either of you recognize this watch?"

"That's mine!" Stewart exclaimed. "I couldn't find it anywhere and thought I'd lost my mind. Where was it?"

"Oh, just laying in the barn aisle," she fibbed, handing it over. "Anyways, it sounds like I need to head back to the house for a nap," she sighed. "I'll call you later if I have any issues."

Chapter 5

Millie tried to fall asleep, but couldn't stop rolling around in her cool sheets. Facing the wall, she pressed her face into the pillow and groaned. After ninety minutes of trying, she supposed it was time to surrender to the fact she would need to rely on caffeine and nerves to keep her awake that night.

Swinging her legs over the side of the bed, she tried to think of productive ways to spend her afternoon. Laundry, dishes, maybe finish unpacking. Her thoughts wandered to her parents guiltily. She had been at Willowmere for a few days, but hadn't done more than send her mother a quick text here and there. To be fair, her mother hadn't reached out either, probably because she was unhappy with Millie's decision to go to Kentucky. They had fought the day before she left, her mother loudly proclaiming that everyone was abandoning her.

As for her father, she wasn't sure what to say to him. He was supportive, but might as well have been in Siberia for how difficult it would be to get ahold of him. Millie felt a deep ache thinking of when she saw him last, just days before he was to embark on the Appalachian Trail, his journey beginning in Maine. "I'm so proud of you," he whispered into her hair when he hugged her at the airport.

Her mother had hugged her too, but it felt distant, her face sagging as she pulled away. "You need to be careful," she told Millie in a tone that sounded more like a threat.

Millie rummaged through her suitcase until she found what she needed, a pen and a generic Kentucky postcard from the airport. Sitting at the modest wooden desk in the corner, she held her pen above the white paper, staring at the blank space. She bit her lip. Where to start? Would he even want to hear about her life while he was immersed in nature?

She took a deep breath and began scrawling.

Dear Dad,

Well, I made it to Willowmere Farm! It's even more beautiful than it looked in the pictures. I'm afraid I still haven't met Richard and Kelly Jennings, the couple that owns the farm. They're away unexpectedly on account of Richard being injured the night before I got here. He was trampled by a loose horse and is under observation at the state hospital in Louisville. Stewart, the Yearling manager who is filling in, said they should be back in a few days.

They had Sloane, their broodmare foreman, pick me up from the airport. I can't say she was overly friendly. Actually, she barely said two words to me the entire ride back! Hopefully she warms up to me soon, as we're supposed to work together in the foaling barn.

Breeding season is in full swing here. It's been crazy busy—from mucking out stalls, to fussing over the expectant mares, it seems there's never a dull moment. New foals are being born almost every night, with many more on their way.

There have been a few strange happenings since I've arrived. Little things mostly, a wasp nest inside the tractor, power to the Foaling Barn being manually turned off in the middle of the night, and of course the creepy graveyard. Last night, the night watchman quit her job halfway through her shift at 3 AM. She apparently claimed the place was haunted or something!

Anyhow, this leads me to some exciting news. Yours truly will be taking over night watch duties until they can find an appropriate replacement! I'm excited for something a little different, but I just can't seem to shake the weird feeling I have about this place. Wish me luck!

Love, Millie

Glancing over her note, she set down her pen and placed the postcard on her nightstand. In the morning, she would drop it in the mail. With a pang of homesickness, she called her mother but it went straight to voicemail.

Millie crossed her arms, shivering as she stepped out the front door.

"I hope you're wearing an extra layer," Jessica advised. "It can be warm during the day, but once the sun goes down it gets cold fast. And I can tell you from experience, the heater in the night watch truck doesn't work all that well."

Millie smiled nervously. "Yes, I'm bringing an extra coat and some snacks. I hope I'm not forgetting anything. I'm so afraid I'll miss something…"

"You'll be fine," Jessica offered sympathetically. "Just watch the foaling mares closely. Once you see one getting ready to foal, it's unmistakable. Everything else should take care of itself. And you can always call me or Stewart if you need help. Okay?"

"Okay," Millie replied hesitantly.

The girls remained silent until they arrived at the foaling barn. Jessica pulled up beside the night watch truck that was parked out front. "You'll be alright, won't you? I know you're new here, but you seem like you have everything under control. Just go inside and touch base with Chloe—she'll be able to tell you if any of the mares are acting strange. I'll come back to do your first lap of the farm with you in about an hour."

Millie strode towards the barn doors, the wind cutting at her face. Inside, Chloe was waiting, car keys in hand. "Hey, how are things going?" Millie asked,

"Everything is quiet for right now. You might keep an eye on Snowy Morning—she was stall walking for a little while, but she's eating hay now."

"Right," Millie replied, nodding her head. "I guess I'll see you again tomorrow?"

"Yeah, I should be here," she nodded. "Good luck, Millie. Don't let the ghosts scare you too much," she teased, walking away without a backward glance.

Millie paced the barn aisle, peering in each stall as she passed. It felt odd to be here by herself after dark, but the mares paid her no attention, contentedly munching on hay.

She was so preoccupied thinking of things she had to do, and all the potential things that could go wrong, that she didn't hear Jessica arrive an hour later. When she called out in greeting, Millie jumped back from the water bucket she was topping off, spilling water all over the aisle. She closed her eyes for a moment and laughed. "Jeepers, you really scared me there!"

Jessica giggled. "Just call me the ghost of Willowmere. Let's get going. The sooner we finish this, the sooner I can go to bed!"

The two girls drove away from the foaling barn, the night only illuminated by the truck's headlights. As they crept along the tree lined drive, Jessica began giving instructions. "You can do things in whatever order you like, but I usually start with the yearling barns, then work my way around the rest of the farm. There are pull off spots on the farm roads where you can use the high beam flashlight to do a headcount. You just want to make sure that the horses are standing up and alive. If one is acting weird—pawing the ground, rolling around, or lifting a leg off the ground, you need to go in and check on them.

"Otherwise, you'll need to keep an eye out for anything in general that looks wrong. The gates are locked 24/7, but you still want to be security conscious. Check the fences as you drive along to make sure they haven't been damaged to the point a horse could escape. Common sense stuff."

"Do I need to go inside the barns during rounds?" Millie asked.

"Only if there are horses inside, unless you need to check something. Right now, most everything is living out except for the foaling mares and a few yearlings, unless there's bad weather predicted. If horses are in, on every round, you'll just stop by the barn and top off the water buckets, and give them breakfast at 6 AM."

"Okay," she said, glancing at the clock on the dashboard. "So, it's 8:15 now... You think I should do rounds again at midnight and 4 AM?"

Jessica nodded and shrugged. "Whatever works for you. The important thing is that you only go if the mares are quiet. If it's midnight and you have a mare pacing and pawing —don't leave her. Either she'll have her foal or she'll cool off, but don't leave a mare unattended if she looks like she's doing something. We do have a webcam set up in most of the Foaling Barn stalls, so if you think someone is close but not imminent, you can always

35

do checks while watching them from your phone."

Millie continued her rounds, driving slowly to make sure she didn't miss anything. With Jessica's help, she found all the watch points for the pastures and used the large flashlight to count out the horses. With all of the horses healthy and accounted for, Millie and Jessica made their way back to the Foaling Barn.

"You all good, Millie?" Jessica asked.

"Yes, I think I've got it all now. Thank you for all your help. I'll see you in the morning!"

A little after midnight, Millie looked over the mares one more time before heading out on her next round of outdoor checks. The mares looked up at her curiously, before lowering their heads back to their hay piles. She lingered for a moment, watching Snowy Morning as she swished her tail in irritation. Millie suspected she would be the next mare to foal. Though she couldn't put her finger on it, the mare was not quite herself, looking around with wide eyes, and stomping her hooves in the deep straw. "You just hang on until I'm back, okay girl?" Snowy just blinked at her with a blank expression.

Millie looked back at the barn before hopping in the night watch truck and turning the ignition. Was it okay to leave her alone? After all, the old mare was not giving any solid signs of impending labor. It was only Millie's personal suspicions that were making her nervous. After a moment of deliberation, Millie pulled out her phone and tapped the security camera app that provided a view of each stall. She selected Snowy's stall number and watched the mare eat hay quietly on the live stream. *I'll just leave that on while I do checks*, she told herself before putting the truck in drive.

Just as she had with Jessica, Millie started with the Yearling

Barns, and worked her way back towards the maiden and retired mares. The horses blinked at her sleepily as she shone her spotlight on them, their lips drooping with drowsiness. All appeared quiet and well.

Glancing at her phone screen as she pulled away, Millie felt a surge of panic. Snowy Morning was laying flat out! Was she foaling?! The video was too grainy to tell for certain.

She was on the opposite side of the farm, but was confident she could make it within five minutes if she drove quickly. Setting her jaw, she gripped the steering wheel and stared straight ahead as she sped along the narrow road. After passing the Yearling Barn, she briefly glanced down at her phone screen to see Snowy still laying flat out, her sides heaving with exertion.

While trying to stay focused on the road, she found Stewart's number in her phone and frantically pressed the call button. Stewart answered quickly. "Hello? Is everything all right?"

"I think Snowy Morning is foaling. I was checking the retired mares and looked at her camera. She's been laying flat out for a few minutes. I'm almost to the barn, I'm going as fast as I can," she blurted out.

"Okay Millie, just relax and I'll be right over," Stewart reassured her, ending the call.

Millie reluctantly slowed down when she got to the four way stop before the foaling barn. Glancing both ways, she pressed the gas pedal and zipped up the hill.

In her rush, she did a double take. The Yearling Barn lights were on, yet Millie knew for certain she had turned them off before leaving earlier that night. Would someone have needed to stop by for something? She glanced at the clock, 12:45 AM. Surely, no one else was at the farm this late. She grimaced, glancing back at the glowing barn before speeding away. She tried to focus on the task at hand, but couldn't help but feel that something was amiss.

"It's a filly," Millie declared excitedly as she heard Stewart's footsteps in the aisle. Once she had sprinted into the barn, there had been no time to waste. Grabbing the foaling supplies and jumping into action, she helped pull the foal out before toweling off the wet newborn.

"Would you look at that," Stewart grinned, "Your first solo foaling, and it looks like everyone came through in good shape. Have you already sprayed her umbilical stump?"

Millie nodded. "Yes, as soon as the umbilical cord tore. Everything happened so fast I didn't even have time to feel nervous. I'm so sorry I almost missed it. I can't believe how quickly it all happened."

Stewart nodded. "Every now and again, even the best run operations can miss one. But if you're paying attention to the signs, like you were, usually you'll catch it in time. And really, for all that can go wrong, mares usually do remarkably well without assistance."

The dark filly extended her front legs, making her first feeble attempts at standing. Snowy lifted her head from the straw, before standing up and taking two large steps towards her newborn daughter. The old mare began to nicker in encouragement as the foal's unsteady legs wobbled and swayed beneath her.

"Should we help?" Millie asked Stewart.

He shook his head. "They'll be fine, I reckon. Snowy is an experienced old mare, she knows to be gentle with the foal. And that filly looks plenty healthy to me. Keep an eye on them to make sure she starts nursing, but otherwise leave them alone tonight."

Millie nodded, leaning on the stall door to watch the mare and foal. As Stewart turned to leave, the night came rushing back to her. "On my way here, I saw the lights were on in the Yearling Barn again. Did you turn them on?"

Stewart furrowed his eyebrows, frowning. "No Millie. I was in bed. Are you sure?"

Millie laughed lightly. "Maybe all this excitement is starting to get to me. You head on and have a good night. I'll call if anything changes."

Millie watched the new foal nurse, then sleepily drop into the straw for the third time. Snowy Morning stood proudly over her daughter, her eyes constantly scanning for potential threats. With the other mares quiet, Millie finally felt comfortable enough to leave for her last round of night check.

Pulling up to the Yearling Barn, all appeared quiet and dark. As Millie walked into the cool concrete block barn, she paused, listening closely. *Water running?* She followed the sound outside, squinting through the darkness. Following the curve of the gravel path leading to one of the filly fields, she scanned her light to the left of the pasture gate. Her gaze landed on a water hydrant with water pouring out.

Millie frowned, and carefully stepped through the mud surrounding the hydrant. *Maybe it's broken,* she considered before attempting to turn the spigot off. Much to her surprise, the pump worked smoothly and the water shut off immediately.

Millie shook her head and turned back to the barn. She briefly glanced in the tack and feed rooms, but seeing nothing of note, she turned the lights out and drove off to complete her checks.

Chapter 6

Morning arrived with a pink streaked sky and the anxious whinnies of mares ready to be turned out for the day. Though tired, Millie felt good about how her first night watch shift had gone. After the hydrant, nothing strange had happened, the horses were fine, and the new foal continued to thrive. She stood in the Foaling Barn doors, anxiously awaiting Jessica, who would bring her back to the house for some breakfast, then much needed sleep.

Jessica drove her car up to Millie and rolled down her window. "Hop in," she called, "Unless you want to stay for the day?" she teased.

Millie laughed. "I'm afraid I don't have the energy for much more than a nap!"

Jessica nodded sympathetically. "I hear you. But it sounded like you had an exciting night at least. A foal your very first night! Stewart said it was a filly?"

"Yes, I thought I was going to have a heart attack when I saw Snowy laying flat out on the video monitor! She did great though, I was already drying the foal off by the time Stewart got there."

After a moment of silence, Millie turned towards Jessica.

"Have you ever seen the Yearling Barn lights turn on without anyone there?"

Jessica appeared puzzled. "No? I can't say that I have. Are you sure no one was there?"

Millie shrugged. "It was after midnight, and Stewart said it wasn't him. But," she began conspiratorially, "When I went back there to check things around 4, I heard water running. I followed the noise, and found one of the pasture hydrants turned on."

"That is weird," Jessica admitted. "I'll ask around today for you, see if anyone else knows anything."

Millie hesitated. "Actually, if you don't mind, I'd rather keep this between you and me. Don't want anyone thinking I'm crazy," she laughed nervously.

Jessica raised her eyebrows. "Okay, whatever you want. I'll keep an ear out though. I heard Eduardo complaining that the fridge and microwave down there kept malfunctioning. Maybe it's somehow related."

Early afternoon light streamed into Millie's bedroom, and she felt a bit like a zombie. After Jessica dropped her off at the house earlier, she had made herself some eggs that tasted like sawdust, took a shower, and collapsed into her bed. She was awoken by the sound of knocking on the door, groaning as she rolled over. "This better be important," she grumbled under her breath, grabbing a hair elastic to tie her hair up into a bun.

Standing at the doorstep was Joe, with a sheepish smile and toolbox in hand. "Sorry if I woke you... Jessica said the washing machine wasn't working? I knew you were on night watch last night, so I didn't want to come in the morning."

Millie self consciously touched her bun, glancing down in

horror at her old flannel pajama pants and oversize t-shirt. Why hadn't she thought to look in the mirror before answering the door? "Come in," she gestured, her cheeks flaming in embarrassment as she led him to the laundry room. *To be fair, I quite literally just rolled out of bed,* she tried to rationalize.

Joe seemed oblivious to her discomfort. He crouched down and started inspecting the machine, pulling tools out of his box. "So," he asked. "How did you like night watch?"

Millie liked watching him work, the crease he got between his eyebrows when he was inspecting something, and how he handled his tools with a practiced ease. She wanted to trust him. "It was fine. A little spooky, to be honest," she admitted. "Snowy Morning had a filly. Easy foaling, so that was good."

Joe nodded. "There have been times I've had to stay at the maintenance building overnight, before a big snow or ice storm. It does feel a little weird after dark, doesn't it? I sure wouldn't be hanging out around that graveyard," he laughed.

Millie smiled. "Are you saying you believe in ghosts, Joe?"

Joe laughed good-naturedly and raised his hands in defeat. "I don't know Millie, I'm inclined to say no but I've seen a strange thing or two in my time here."

"Like what?" she pressed.

"You're going to think I'm crazy," he countered.

Millie shook her head. "Never."

"When I was living in the other house down this road, about a year ago? I came home after work one day, and all the pictures on the wall had been rearranged. I didn't have roommates at that point, so I had a bit of an existential crisis for a day, wondering if I had truly lost my mind. There were a few other little things too, nothing major. Silverware in random places, stuff like that."

"Were there any signs that someone broke in?" Millie asked, fascinated.

Joe shrugged. "I couldn't find any signs of forced entry. I sure wasn't going to call the police because someone shuffled around my pictures, so I tried to forget about it. At the end of last year I got my own apartment, and that was the end of it."

"You didn't like living on the farm?"

"I wasn't crazy about everyone on the farm knowing when I was coming and going. When you live on site, no one has any qualms about calling you on your day off." He cleared his throat, looking embarrassed. "Not that there's anything wrong with living here. It just wasn't for me."

"I can understand that," Millie contemplated. "It's fine temporarily, but I don't know if I would like it long term either. The upside to this over a rental is that I can just walk to work, if Jessica can't give me a ride for some reason."

"How long are you planning to be here then?" he asked, glancing back at her.

"I'm not sure, to be honest. At least through the end of June. The Jennings' said I could stay on for yearling prep through the summer if I wanted, but I haven't made up my mind yet."

Joe stood up and gathered his tools. "Well, tell Jessica to call me if it stops working again."

"Of course," Millie nodded, leading him to the door.

"Millie," he said, pausing in the doorway. "I wouldn't mind one bit if you decided to stay on for the summer."

Millie bit her lip and smiled. She closed the door gently, pausing to stare down at the laminate wood floor. "I need to go back to bed," she grumbled to herself, shaking her head.

"You would just love it here," Becca gushed. "I really wish you were here!"

Millie sighed into the phone. "I know. I'm learning so much here, but I miss you and Callie. Maybe over the summer I can make a quick visit."

"Yes, with all your spare time Millie! I'm so glad you thought to call me. I've been wanting to talk, but the time zones just mess everything up."

"I know, I never thought I would be happy about being up after midnight! I'm so glad I remembered that you're eight hours behind me. You wouldn't believe some of the things happening here. It's kind of making me wonder."

"Like what? Now you have me intrigued."

"Well, before I even got here, Richard Jennings, who owns the farm with his wife? He got trampled by some colts that were set loose after dark. Then, my first day here, the foaling barn foreman was attacked by a swarm of wasps.

"That night, as a mare was foaling, the power to the Foaling Barn appears to have been deliberately turned off. *Then*, the night watchman, Connie, quit without notice on account of the farm being 'haunted'!"

"Sounds like you've been busy," she laughed. "You don't really think the farm is haunted though, do you?" Becca asked.

"I'm skeptical, but things keep getting stranger. When the power went out the other night, I noticed all the Yearling Barn lights were on though the barn was empty. Then late last night, the barn got lit up again, even though no one was supposed to be there.

"When I went to investigate, someone had turned on the water outside and left it running. And Joe told me when he lived here, somehow all the pictures in his house got rearranged! I don't buy the supernatural angle, but something odd is going on here."

"Joe?" Becca inquired. "Who is he? Is he cute?"

Millie sighed in exasperation. "Joe works in maintenance, Becca."

"And?" Becca prodded further.

"He's working on his engineering degree when he's not working. He's very nice. And yeah, he isn't too hard on the eyes," Millie laughed.

"This is perfect," Becca replied smugly. "A whirlwind romance will take your mind off any ghosts that may or may not be haunting this amazing farm you've found yourself on. There has to be a logical explanation somewhere for all of it."

"Becca, there will be no 'whirlwind romance' in my life anytime soon. And there *is* a strange vibe here, but I admit I may be overthinking things."

"Then keep your head down and do a little investigating on your own," Becca encouraged. "Do you have any idea why all this might be happening?"

"No," Millie said thoughtfully. "I don't know what the possible motive would be. After the wasp attack, I did find a watch in the tractor, and a lighter in a stall with the initials JMD. Stewart claimed the watch, but I don't know who the lighter belongs to."

"All you can do is keep your ears open. And please, be careful."

"I will. My phone is almost dead, and I can't find my charger anywhere, so I should probably get going. I'll keep you posted on what's going on."

The two friends exchanged goodbyes, and Millie sat deep in thought for several minutes. Becca and her twin sister Callie were a year older than her, and had taken a gap year after graduating high school the prior year. Millie had always thought of them like the big sisters she never had. But they had barely spoken since she turned down a trip to Ireland with them earlier that year. Outwardly, they were supportive, but Millie got the sense they didn't understand why she had gone to Kentucky. Sometimes she wondered too.

With a sigh, she stood, walking one round of the barn to make sure the mares were settled. She then began her drive to the Yearling Barn.

Millie flipped the light switch in the empty barn, noting the eerie silence. The map in the maintenance building had been bothering her, and she figured now was as good a time as any to investigate further.

She walked to the side of the barn behind the feed room, and turned on her dying cell phone light, searching for any abnormalities or disruptions on the surface of the barn walls. After several minutes of looking, she stepped back, disappointed. If there had been an additional tack room on the side of the barn, it was long gone.

She walked back up the barn aisle, peeking in at the tack and storage rooms. Before walking outside to check the hydrant she had turned off the night prior, she pushed the partially open feed room door. "What on earth..." Millie muttered under her breath. The full feed bins had all their lids flipped up, leaving the sweet smelling grain available to any mice or raccoons that happened to stumble across it. Millie knew that this could potentially ruin the feed, either from the vermin spreading disease, or raccoons completely ransacking the place.

She shook her head and began closing and latching each lid. On the final bin, she did a double take. Sitting on top of the molasses coated grain, was her very distinctive hot pink phone charger. Millie felt her stomach drop, and she glanced back over her shoulder.

She squinted through the darkness as she walked out to the filly field, listening closely for the sound of running water. There was only silence.

Sensing her presence, two yearling fillies marched up, hooking their heads over the fence. "Hey girls," Millie smiled, reaching her hand up to play with the chestnut's forelock, before the bay pushed her aside. After a moment, both fillies froze, their nostrils flaring as they looked back. "What do you guys see out there?"

The two fillies took off like a shot across the pasture, the rest of the herd trailing behind. As Millie was turning to leave, she saw it—a tall figure walked across the middle of the field, glowing in a silver light.

Chapter 7

Millie knelt down, crawling into the bushes in hopes the darkness would hide her. A wave of fear rose up in her stomach as she continued watching. Her mind darted in a million different directions—should she run for safety? Play possum in the bushes?

The ghostly figure strode up to the gate, heading straight towards the bushes where she was hidden. She tensed in horror—could it see her?! Holding her breath, she remained crouched down as the gate creaked open.

All she could see was the ghost's lace up work boots moving across the ground. They headed up the gravel path to the barn, their relaxed gait leading her to believe they weren't interested in hunting her down, even if they could see her.

Millie sat motionless for several minutes, before she heard a loud scratching sound come from the barn. Her spine tensed and she gritted her teeth, remaining silent.

A moment later, footsteps approached again, opening and shutting the gate, before striding off towards a large oak tree in the middle of the field. Before Millie could see where they were going, they disappeared.

She stood carefully, looking around nervously. On the gravel path, there was a shallow boot print, only a bit larger than her own. The footprint could have belonged to anyone, but if it *was* the ghost, she bet it was a woman.

Millie knew she had been gone too long and hoped that the expecting mares were still okay. Flipping the barn lights off and running out to the night watch truck, she turned the key in the ignition. As the truck roared to life, the headlights illuminated the barn doors ahead. Millie saw what had caused the scratching sound. Across the front of the barn was a jagged message: LEAVE THIS FARM NOW

"Good morning," Jessica chirped. "Everything was quiet last night?"

Millie nodded, deep in thought. She hesitated to confide in Jessica, but knew there were going to be questions when everyone saw the scratched out message. "Has anyone ever mentioned the Yearling Barn being a little... weird?"

"What is this about the Yearling Barn again?" Jessica asked, exasperated. "What do you mean?"

"Someone—or *something*—scratched out a pretty ominous message on the barn doors. Right before, I had thought I'd seen something glowing out in the field. Whatever it was, it sure spooked the fillies."

Jessica shook her head, her expression skeptical. "Look, I'm not trying to start anything. But are you *certain* about what you saw?"

"What does *that* mean?" Millie retorted. "Do you not believe me? Because feel free to go look at the barn doors yourself, the evidence is plain as day."

Jessica took a deep breath. "I'm not saying I don't believe you. Just that there have been some questions raised."

"What kind of questions?"

"Well," Jessica began, sputtering on her words. "I don't want to get into it. Just please be careful with how much you talk about this haunting stuff."

Jessica's non answer aggravated Millie even more. "You've lost me," she replied curtly.

"Have you told Stewart yet?"

Millie shook her head. "Honestly, I've been trying to figure out how to tell him without sounding a bit off my rocker. But I guess this is just the latest in the series of recent events."

Jessica frowned. "It does seem like a lot of things are going wrong around here lately. But I can't imagine anything is behind it. The farm is just experiencing a bit of bad luck," she nodded with affirmation.

"Right," Millie replied without conviction.

"This glowing thing you saw—if it will make you feel better, this afternoon I'll drive you out to that field. I'm sure it was just fireflies or something, but we can check it out."

Millie nodded in appreciation, but knew Jessica didn't really understand what she was saying. They parted ways at the house, agreeing that Jessica would pick her back up at 4 o'clock. "Just as soon as work is over, there shouldn't be anyone around to bother us." Jessica reassured her.

Once Millie was inside alone, she kicked off her leather paddock boots and moved about the kitchen, gathering eggs and milk to make herself breakfast. Her phone began to vibrate and she grimaced, knowing it was likely Stewart.

"Hello?" she answered cautiously.

"Millie—what happened last night at the Yearling Barn?"

Millie took a deep breath and recounted the story. "I know how it sounds. Something or someone knew I was in that barn, and wanted to send a message. The person—I think it was a woman—was dressed in a glowing white gown, wandering around the yearling filly pasture. They went to the barn, and when I came back after they left, the message was there. I don't know why, or exactly what it means, but something is off at this farm Stewart. If you have any ideas, I'd love to hear them."

Stewart sounded disbelieving. "That sounds like the Lockhurst Lady. But that's just an old myth."

"The Lockhurst Lady?" Millie asked. "Who is that?"

"Legend has it that the ghost of Sarah Lockhurst can be seen floating about the farm, attacking unattended children. The version I've heard around the campfire is that she came back to seek revenge for the decrepit old tobacco barn being torn down. Personally, I think the grooms were just using it as a convenient story to tell the farm kids so they didn't wander into the pastures."

"Lockhurst?" Millie mused, "Is she buried up in the graveyard? I think I saw that surname up there."

"I suppose it's possible, if she was a real person. I've never had much reason to do any research."

"Was she ever seen by the Yearling Barn?" Millie inquired.

"Not to my knowledge? Honestly I only heard a few secondhand stories about her and I thought they were completely made up. Jeffrey, the man who told one of them, was a terrible alcoholic. We always joked that he imagined her after drinking one night."

"Does he still work here?" Millie asked.

"No, he left about a year ago. I think he works at Skyfront Farm now."

"Do you think he would be willing to speak with me?"

Stewart sighed. "I'm not sure you fully understand how things work in this town. We cannot have word getting out about what's going on here. Clients would start taking their mares to other farms to foal, and no one would want their horses getting prepped for the yearling sales here. It's best for everyone if this all stays within the farm."

Millie fought to keep her voice steady. "I understand, Stewart. However, I would think if you truly cared about the future of the farm, you would want to find out why these things are happening. Sweeping it under the rug won't get us to the bottom of anything."

"Are you insinuating that I don't want to know what's going on here?" Stewart growled.

"Not at all," Millie said sweetly. "I just want to make sure this is being looked at from all different angles."

"That's not your job to worry about, Millie."

"At least promise me that you'll tell the Jennings' about all of this when they get back? They deserve to know. I know there's not enough to go to the police or anything, but they might want to increase security, set up more cameras."

There was a long pause. "You're right Millie. As soon as they're back, I will tell them myself. But until then, please keep this to yourself?"

"Of course," she replied. "You have my word."

After they said goodbye, Millie hung up and stood at the kitchen counter, drumming her fingers. Did Stewart have something to hide?

Come afternoon, the air was hot and cloying, Millie squinting against the sun. She fanned her face with her hand, her thighs sticking uncomfortably to the seat of the golf cart. "Filly field at the Yearling Barn, right?" Jessica asked over the noise of the golf cart.

"Yep," Millie confirmed. It felt as if every limb in her body was begging her to go back to bed, her eyes scratchy and feet heavy. After she spoke with Stewart, she ate breakfast, did laundry, and cleaned the kitchen. Then before she knew it, Jessica was home waking her up. *Maybe Jessica has some energy drinks stashed somewhere for tonight*, she thought numbly.

Jessica slammed on the brakes, snapping Millie out of her daydream. "Just tell me where you want me to go," Jessica hollered as Millie opened the pasture gate.

Millie scanned the pasture. "Try driving straight ahead to the middle," she suggested. "When we get to the spot where I saw the figure, we can take a look around on foot. I want to see if they left anything behind."

It didn't take long for the curious yearling fillies to notice the girls driving. To them, a golf cart driving in their pasture meant one thing, meal time! Though they had already eaten dinner, the fillies circled the golf cart, pressing their noses to the windshield. "I guess we're stuck here," Jessica laughed.

"This actually should work fine," Millie said, noting that this was near where she had seen the Lockhurst Lady walking. "If we can ever get past all these fillies!"

The two girls carefully pushed their way through the crowd of ten hungry horses, offering scratches and pats as an apology for not having treats to give. "You walk left, I'll go right," Millie suggested. "Just try to keep an eye out for anything that shouldn't be here. Scraps of clothing, obvious footprints, anything really."

Jessica nodded and they went their separate ways. Millie carefully examined the ground with every step, but found nothing of note. A lanky chestnut broke off from the herd to follow her. Millie glanced down at her hooves, and realized with disappointment that footprints or clues would have been trampled by hooves in the night. She sighed and glanced at the filly who stretched her nose out curiously. "What do you think?" Millie asked, running her fingers though the filly's neatly pulled mane. "What did you see last night, huh?"

"Hey!" Jessica shouted from about five hundred feet away. "I think I found something!"

Millie strode over to the patch of leaf covered earth that Jessica was standing over. "Look!" Jessica said with urgency, as she carefully kicked back some leaves, revealing mesh fishnet material.

Millie frowned. "Be careful. I'll be right back." She went to a tree surrounded by a fence and climbed through. As she had hoped, there was a long branch inside the pen that she grabbed and dragged back to Jessica. The fillies snorted, jumping back in fear. "It's just a branch, silly girls,"

Millie carefully used the branch to push back the leaves, revealing more mesh. "Millie?" Jessica inquired. "Why do you think this is out here? We've got to pull it out, if a horse ate that it could be fatal—"

Jessica broke off her sentence and stared in disbelief as Millie threw the entire branch into the center of the leaf patch. When the branch hit, it disappeared from view, falling down into a deep hole, the fine mesh breaking to line the sides of the hole.

"It was a trap," Millie said grimly. "Notice, that ditch is the perfect size for a horse."

Jessica's face was ashen as she fumbled for her phone. "This is not good Millie. If one of those fillies had run over those leaves..."

Millie nodded solemnly, glancing back at the fillies who were now grazing peacefully. She didn't need Jessica to finish the sentence to know what she meant. The list of potential injuries were endless, many ending in an early demise for a promising young horse. Millie shivered. If she had wanted to find out what was behind the strange happenings before, now she had a steely determination.

Jessica frantically spoke into her phone, Millie unsure if she was talking to Stewart or had called the Jennings'. There was a long pause as she took a deep breath. "Okay, we'll do that."

Jessica ended the call and turned to Millie. "Stewart wants us to bring the fillies into the barn. He's going to call maintenance back in to bring dirt to fill in the hole. They'll check the rest of the field too. You'll have to turn them back out on night watch tonight."

Millie nodded, remaining silent, her mind considering all possible angles as they led the young horses into the barn. Did the Lockhurst Lady make an appearance last night in hopes of spooking the horses so one of them would fall into the trap? Millie shivered. She would call Becca later to share her latest theory. For now, she decided to keep it to herself.

Chapter 8

All was quiet and well in the foaling barn when Millie began her shift. Seven Wonders had foaled a small chestnut filly two hours prior. The foal looked strong and healthy, already walking around and nursing as her dam watched her fondly. With only the sound of happy horses nickering in greeting, and no mares currently waxing, Millie left to turn out the yearling fillies.

In the Yearling Barn, the fillies whinnied anxiously, spinning around in their stalls. Coming in for the afternoon was unusual for them, and they seemed eager to vocalize their discontent. Lenny Penny, a muscular blood bay pawed at her stall door, every muscle tensed. "Easy girl," Millie cooed, laying a gentle hand on her neck as she clipped the lead rope to her halter. The filly pranced and arched her neck towards Millie as they marched to her pasture. As soon as Millie faced her to the gate and released her, she charged off at a strong gallop, never looking back towards the barn.

One after another, the fillies were turned out, each one practically exploding with excitement upon release. The tenth and final filly, Singing Bells, was no exception until Millie released her. Instead of running, she stretched her nose to the ground and snorted, her body quivering with excitement. Millie looked around curiously. "What are you looking at, pretty girl?"

With a rustle in the bushes next to the gate, a fluffy calico cat emerged. "Well hello there," Millie smiled, crouching down to stroke the cat. "Where did you come from?"

The cat blinked at Millie before ducking under the gate and trotting forward several steps. Singing Bells, clearly bored by this new development, walked off lazily towards her herd. The cat paused and looked back at Millie with an annoyed expression. *Meowwwww*, the cat howled, staring Millie in the eye.

"What?" Millie asked the cat. "Are you asking me to follow you?"

Feeling quite foolish, she followed the cat's black and orange feather duster tail into the pasture. The cat moved forward with confidence, only pausing to check that Millie was still following. *This is crazy*, she told herself as she stepped through the tall grass.

Finally, the calico darted under a fence surrounding a magnificent oak tree. Millie peered over the fence and watched its tail disappear as it darted through a hole at the base. A second later, the cat's white head popped out of the hole, letting out a soft mew.

"Is this where you live? Why are you all the way out here?" she asked.

Millie crouched down to examine the hole, scratching the cat's chin to placate it. She turned on her cell phone flashlight and shone it around the inside of the tree. It appeared to be almost entirely hollow. Stranger yet, she could see two cat bowls sitting inside. She stood up and walked around the tree, her eyes scanning for any man made marks in the wood.

Seeing nothing, she stretched her hand inside the cat hole and felt around, landing on a long metal object. *A lever?* Millie pulled downward, flinching in surprise at the loud creak. A tight fitting door, with rough edges to disguise itself appeared, swinging outward. She looked both ways nervously to be sure no one was watching, then stepped inside, the calico cat still twirling around her ankles.

Inside the tree was barely large enough for Millie, cramped and smelling of wet earth and old wood. Next to the feed and water dish was a small plastic container filled with cat food, and a twelve pack of bottled water next to it. She only scooped a small amount of food and water into the bowls. "I just don't want to tip off whoever is taking care of you, that's all," she explained apologetically. "But I can come back to check on you sometime. Okay?"

The cat spun around and left the tree, flicking her tail in irritation. Millie's eyes followed her out, and landed on a small trap door in the center of the floor. Her pulse pounded in her ears as she lifted the rope handle and peered down into darkness.

As Millie lowered herself down the ladder attached to the wall, she felt as if she was in a trance. The glow of her cell phone had allowed her to see a light switch directly under the trapdoor. Now turned on, it provided a dull, yellow light and a constant buzzing sound.

At the bottom of the ladder, she looked around. *I guess this must be a tunnel of some sort,* she considered. The path was narrow, walls lined with mossy stones, and a dirt floor. Millie nervously checked her phone, surprised to see she still had service and was able to glance at the foaling cameras. With the mares all appearing content, she knew there was only one thing to do.

Millie forged ahead as the tunnel narrowed. Throwing a nervous glance back, the ladder grew smaller behind her before disappearing around a curve. As she walked, she tried to think about where she must be under the farm. Perhaps this was leading her back towards the road? Millie grimaced as her cell phone vibrated in her pocket, and let out a breath of relief when she saw it was Becca calling. "Hey Becca, you're never going to believe where I'm at."

"Oh, I don't know," Becca teased. "Mucking a stall? Scrubbing a water trough? Pulling a mane?"

Millie laughed. "Clearly you haven't completely forgotten your grooming days."

"Never! I may spend my weekends getting manicures now, but I do still have horses in my blood!" Becca retorted back. "But seriously, what's going on? You on a hot date with Joe?"

"A hot date?!" Millie sputtered out. "As if! I'll give you one more guess."

Becca sighed into the phone. "I don't know Millie, horse farm life can be so... predictable. My final guess is waiting around on some poor old pregnant mare to have her baby!"

"Not even close," Millie said. "I'll tell you, but you have to promise not to tell your parents. If my mom found out, she would get me out of here faster than I could say 'Foaling season.'"

Becca giggled. "Don't tell me you're in a club. Or better yet, at Joe's house? Speaking of that, has he asked you out yet?"

Millie sighed in exasperation as she continued walking. "It's so much better than that. I found an underground tunnel!"

"Like, a tourist attraction? I've heard Mammoth Cave is amazing," Becca enthused.

"No, no," Millie explained. "I'm on the farm in an underground tunnel! I have no idea if anyone else even knows this exists," she continued.

"Does anyone know you're down there?" Becca pressed, concerned. "That sounds really unsafe, Millie."

"Well, no, not exactly. But it has electricity and is well constructed, just old." Millie retorted defensively.

"I don't like the sound of this," Becca declared. "You need to leave and not go back."

Millie pursed her lips and inwardly sighed. She adored her best friend, but hated when she spoke to her like this. Like Millie was still a shy and awkward girl of nine, unable to make her own decisions. "SHHHHHHHH," Millie hissed between her teeth, mimicking static.

"Millie? Are you still there?"

"CCCKKKKKKKKKK," Millie continued. She covered the speaker of her phone with one hand. "Becca? SHHHHHHHHH. I'm—CKKKKKK—Still here—"

Millie tapped the end call button with a smirk of satisfaction. She was feeling like the tunnel was close to its destination, as the path began to twist and turn and narrow further, until Millie was having to crouch to walk through. She needed her full attention right now, not to be distracted by Becca's older sibling complex.

Anxiously, she checked the foaling barn camera again. She was most concerned about Vallila, a leggy liver chestnut. Millie noted she was eating hay quietly, but was shifting her weight back and forth on each hind leg, occasionally raising one up to kick at her stomach. Labor didn't appear imminent, but Millie knew she needed to hurry and get back to the foaling barn before the mare progressed further. *Just another five minutes,* she thought to herself, not quite ready to turn back.

Millie's heart caught in her throat as she rounded another turn. A ladder leading up to a small door stood fifty feet away, almost identical to the ones at the entrance. She eagerly climbed the ladder and paused at the top, listening carefully for sounds of activity on the other side of the door. Hearing nothing, she opened the door and pulled herself through.

Chapter 9

Millie half expected to end up inside of another tree, but was surprised to find herself inside a crawlspace. Looking up at the low ceiling, she knew would have to crawl on her knees to explore. Wrinkling her nose at the dirty floor, she dodged beams and hoped to avoid rodents and spiders. She wasn't sure where she was going, but gamely crawled ahead, holding her cell phone between her teeth to show the way. She made her way to a large hole in the wall that led to a basement.

Millie dropped down through the hole, and walked towards a stairwell. She tugged on a long string, and was rewarded a bright light filling the entire room. A brief look around showed nothing of note—old paint cans, saw horses, and rusty nails. Knowing she was below a house, she listened closely for any sign they were home. She crept up the stairs cautiously, turning the knob slowly to open the door. She blinked at the sudden brightness, noting the stark silence of the house.

She kicked off her shoes at the top of the stairwell. It wasn't like she was going to be able to make a quick getaway anyways, she reasoned, might as well not mess up the polished hardwood. Millie padded left into a tidy sitting area with pale furniture.

Glancing out the window, a wave of realization hit her—she was in the farm manager's house!

Millie panicked, her chest tightening with fear. The Jennings' were still away, but what if they had cameras? What if they somehow found out she was snooping in their house?! Millie knew it would be virtually impossible to explain.

As quickly as she could, she went back to the basement door, pulled her boots on and headed back to the tunnel. Her heart still racing with adrenaline, she pulled her phone out to observe the cameras as she walked. Vallila was now pawing at the ground, circling the stall with anxious snorts. Millie broke into a jog, time was of the essence now. *If I don't make it back before she breaks water, I'm definitely going to be told to leave...*

Millie peeled the night watch truck out of the yearling barn with a squeal of the tires and headed to the foaling barn. Stealing glances at the camera on her phone, she saw Vallila lay down, steam rising off her back. She pressed down on the gas as hard as she dared, and called Stewart. "Vallila is going now," she blurted out.

"I'll be right over." Stewart responded before hanging up.

When Millie arrived at the foaling barn, she sprinted out of the truck and ran for a foaling kit in the tack room. She was desperate to hide that she had nearly missed the mare foaling, and worked as quickly as she could to wrap Vallila's tail. "Come on girl," Millie said between gritted teeth as she pulled on the mare's halter. She hadn't broken water yet, but it was obvious birth was imminent by her labored breathing and sweaty hide as she laid flat out in the straw. Millie continued tugging, she needed the mare to stand back up so she could move her to the larger foaling stall.

Finally, with Millie's loud urging, the mare pulled herself up, her eyes wide with fear as her water broke. Millie laid a hand on Vallila's hot neck and dragged her to the foaling stall, thankful that it was only across the aisle. The mare collapsed against the wall banked with straw, and Millie dove right in to assist. It wasn't until the head and shoulders were out that she glanced up and noticed Stewart watching. She shook her head in surprise—*How does he appear so quietly?* She rubbed the limp, wet newborn with a towel, trying to coax it into life. After a few moments that felt more like hours, the foal began to draw in deep breaths, its bony rib cage expanding and contracting.

Vallila released the rest of the foal and lifted her head so she could look back at her newborn. Millie smiled as the foal stretched out its nose towards its mother—a long, crooked stripe, like their dam. A quick peek under the tail confirmed it was a colt. The Jennings' would be pleased.

"Colt?" Stewart asked.

Millie nodded, and stood to retrieve an enema from the foaling kit.

Stewart gave her an appraising look. "Doing a lot of digging?" he asked.

Millie was startled. "What?" she asked, glancing down at her clothes in horror—they were covered in dust and dirt. "I... tripped."

Stewart shrugged and raised an eyebrow. "I'm going to head back to the house if you've got this under control. Just make sure you document when he nurses."

"Of course. I'll give you a call if there are any issues." Millie replied, fighting to keep her voice level.

After Stewart had left and she had dried off the shaking newborn, Millie let out a long sigh and slid down the wall, a wave of exhaustion rolling over her. Vallila stood with a loud groan and immediately made her way to stand over her newborn, licking his soft fur and offering whickers of encouragement as he began to unravel his spindly legs.

"I don't know about you," she muttered to the mare. "But I think I've had enough excitement for tonight."

Millie awoke to the sound of rain drumming on the metal roof. She lay under the covers, wondering what her next move should be. She had not told anyone besides Becca about the secret tunnel. A sense of worry gnawed at her—should she at least tell the Jennings'? It was their house, after all.

But how would she be able to explain finding it? And why did she even walk through the tunnel when she was supposed to be working? It seemed to Millie that bringing it up would lead to many unwanted questions.

She heard noise from the kitchen and remembered it was Jessica's day off. *Maybe I can convince her to do some investigating with me,* Millie wondered. She swung her legs off the bed and stretched, suddenly knowing her ambition for the day.

Jessica looked surprised as Millie entered the kitchen. "I didn't expect to see you up so early."

Millie stifled a yawn. "I took a nap but I'm going to try to stay awake the rest of the day so I can sleep tonight. Stewart said he was able to reach an agreement with Connie, so I can go back to working days tomorrow."

Jessica nodded enthusiastically. "That will be great. Eduardo just quit yesterday, so Chloe got stuck with the yearlings."

"Where do you think they'll put me? Back with the foaling mares?"

Jessica nodded. "I think Sloane is back today, my guess is

you'll be working with her."

Millie tried to swallow her disappointment—she loved the mares and foals, but felt like an intruder in Sloane's barn. "Well, at least it will be a good learning experience. I hope."

Jessica snorted with laughter. "Don't sound so excited!"

Millie felt embarrassed at her slip up. "I'm sorry, I'm just tired—"

"It's fine, Millie," the older girl cut her off. "You're not the only one who doesn't love working with Sloane. Actually, that's probably why you're stuck with her, pretty much everyone else on the farm has threatened to quit over her."

"Really?" Millie asked, taken aback. "Why?"

"She's not exactly little miss sunshine, if you haven't noticed," she offered dryly. "She has a tendency to walk off for imaginary duties, like running to the office, or doing inventory, right when an unpleasant task is about to begin. She's not a big fan of cleaning stalls, or manual labor in general."

"Then why hasn't she been fired?"

"It's impossible to find help these days. Why else would an intern be left alone to do night watch and foal mares? No offense to you," she added hastily. "Plus, for being a bit... gruff, Sloane does make sure everything is up to a certain standard. She's a good horseman and very reliable, which counts for a lot."

"I get it," Millie considered. "When you get down to it, people aren't just good or bad, usually they fall somewhere in the middle. If you have someone who cares about the horses and shows up, who cares about the other stuff, right?"

"Now you're thinking like a manager," Jessica smiled.

"Are you doing anything for your day off?" Millie inquired.

"I don't have any plans. We could go out for lunch, if you

wanted."

She didn't want to seem too excited, but inwardly Millie was dying to get off the farm. Though her time on the farm had been interesting, she was eager to explore Lexington more. "That would be fun. Do you have anywhere in mind?"

"If we went to Breezy Knoll, I could drive you by some of the other farms around here," Jessica replied thoughtfully. "It's in an old general store, very cozy. They also sell jams and knick knacks from local artists."

Millie nodded with enthusiasm. "Could we leave early and drive around a bit? I feel like I haven't seen Lexington at all since I've been here. I would love to get the lay of the land out here, but it's hard since I don't have my own car."

"Of course! And I keep forgetting to tell you, but if you need to run to the store or anything, you can always use one of the farm trucks here. The Jennings' don't mind if staff borrow them, just as long as you ask and are not gone long."

"I'll probably take them up on that at some point," she replied, quietly thinking how well that boded for her investigation.

"Is this it?" Millie asked in surprise.

"Yep," Jessica smiled. "I told you it was quaint, didn't I?"

The restaurant sat at the corner of a 4-way stop, looking like a little red ranch house. You would think someone lived there if not for the sign, declaring it as Breezy Knoll Market.

Inside, jockey silks from local farms hung on the wall and worn leather halters from famous stallions were displayed in shadow boxes. Despite being cramped, the hardwood floors and large windows lent a warmth to the small space.

"You have to order a bourbon chocolate milkshake," Jessica advised. "Your Kentucky experience won't be complete without trying it."

"There's no real bourbon in it though, right?"

Jessica laughed. "You didn't think I was trying to get you tipsy, did you? It's just made with crushed up bourbon flavored chocolates."

As the two girls sat down at a table they had claimed, a tall brown haired man approached. "Jessica!" he exclaimed with a broad smile. "It's been too long. How have you been?"

Jessica stood up to hug the man. "I'm so happy to see you. I need to introduce you to my friend Millie. She's our newest intern at Willowmere."

The man smiled broadly and reached out to shake Millie's hand. "What a pleasure, Millie. I'm Alan, Jessica's uncle."

"Lovely to meet you," Millie smiled.

"Please, sit with us!" Jessica exclaimed. "Alan is a bloodstock agent," she divulged. "I'm sure he would be happy to explain the business to you, seeing as you are in Kentucky to learn about the Thoroughbred industry."

Alan smiled good-naturedly. "I actually need to run to meet with a client. Do you girls have plans for later this afternoon?"

Jessica and Millie shrugged at each other, shaking their heads.

"If you would be interested in learning a bit about what I do, I'm supposed to go to Fairdale Stable this afternoon to assess some yearlings. Would you like to join me?"

Millie nodded enthusiastically. "I would love that, if it's not too much trouble,"

"No, not at all Millie. Jessica is always begging me to take her to inspect horses anyways. This should satisfy her for a short while, I hope."

Jessica laughed. "If I had known you were so willing to teach interns, I would've brought you one a long time ago!"

"Anyways," Alan began scribbling on the back of a paper menu. "Here is the address. My appointment is at 2 o'clock. If I'm not at the gate when you arrive, just wait so we can go in together."

Jessica craned her neck as she looked at the address. "The old Marsella Stables? I didn't even know there were horses there now," Jessica said, wrinkling her nose in distaste.

Alan shook his head in warning. "Beggars can't be choosers, Jessica. I'm told there's a Pistol Run filly that's very nice."

Jessica grimaced. "I can't wait to see."

Chapter 10

Millie enjoyed the view from the passenger's side window. The two girls had killed time by wandering around downtown Lyon, a town neighboring Lexington. Though charming, the town had a depressed feel, evidenced by several empty storefronts on Main street.

Millie's appreciation for the area grew as they drove into the countryside. Old oak trees stood strong and tall, their branches twisting and twirling towards the sky. Rolling fields lined with stone walls were greening up with the promise of spring.

"Nice, isn't it?" Jessica asked, glancing over from the steering wheel at Millie.

"It's gorgeous," Millie admitted.

"Lyon does have some of the most fertile soil in Kentucky. Good grass builds good racehorses. I think you'll be disappointed as we get closer to where we're going though."

The car slowed and Jessica flipped her turn signal on. "Here we go," she announced, turning onto Rutherford Road.

Millie carefully studied her surroundings as they crept down the road, noting horses in dirt fields. "Does grass not grow very well out here?" Millie wondered aloud.

Jessica shook her head. "No, you see how many horses are out there? At least a dozen. It's just over grazed here—too many horses, and not enough space. Land is expensive, most of these farms can't rotate horses into different areas to help the ground recover. You see, even where it looks green, it's just weeds."

Millie furrowed her eyebrows. "Does that affect the horses? Don't they need grass?"

Jessica shrugged. "Depends who you ask. There's a reason why Willowmere spends thousands every year just on grass fertilizer. Some people, like the Jennings', believe good grass will result in a stronger, faster racehorse. In all reality, as long as those horses are getting grain and hay so they don't get skinny, they should be fine without any grass.

"But," she added, "In a sport determined by fractions of a second, every extra bit can help. It's almost a status symbol in these parts. City folk argue about who has the best lawn, we fight about who has the best pastures."

They continued down the road, Millie noting rotting old barns and fragile, warped fencing. Though they were only twenty minutes away from Willowmere, Millie felt a thousand miles away.

Jessica flipped the turn signal and turned onto an uneven gravel drive. "Here we are," Jessica announced unceremoniously. She stopped the car out front of the gate, Marsella Stables etched in tired stone. Jessica put her phone to her ear. "How far are you? We just got here."

Jessica sighed loudly. "For real?"

Millie turned her head and listened intently, while Jessica's frown lines deepened. "Okay. I'll touch base with you after we leave then... Yep. Bye now."

Jessica turned to look at Millie. "Change of plans. Uncle Alan isn't coming, he got called away about a sick foal. So it's just going to be me and you, acting as his 'agents', taking pictures and notes of each horse."

"But how will we know what to write?" Millie asked worriedly. "And won't the owner wonder where Alan is?"

Jessica shrugged. "Being a bloodstock assistant isn't *that* hard—just note which horses are really nice or of really poor quality, and take lots of pictures. The truth is, Alan would be here if it was that important. He would never miss a big farm."

Millie was puzzled. "If he doesn't think this farm is important, why did he plan to come in the first place?"

"You just never know where a great horse could come from. Sure, we can make educated guesses based on the pedigree, but part of Alan's job is trying to find diamonds in the rough. Maybe this farm doesn't have great mares, but if they breed to great stallions, the foals could take after the sire."

The car bumped down the narrow drive, until they pulled up to an ancient looking black barn.

Millie hopped out of the car and stared up at it, noting the gaps in the wood panels. "You see the gaps in the wood, Millie? That's an old tobacco barn. The gaps are to encourage airflow so the tobacco could dry faster."

Millie nodded. Without being told, she could see this was a very different sort of farm from Willowmere. Horses stood together in small paddocks, with long unkempt manes and patchy coats. Fence boards were broken and it lacked the manicured aesthetic of Willowmere. A small man with graying hair and worn skin walked out of the barn. "Ladies," he greeted them with a wide smile. "Will Alan be arriving separately?"

Jessica stretched her hand out and began speaking in an authoritative tone. "Jessica Howell. I'm afraid an emergency came up, so Alan won't be joining us. He sent me and my assistant Millie, in his place."

The man furrowed his eyebrows. "Well that's certainly a shame. I had some young stock I was excited to show him. In any case, I'm Riley McConnell."

"Not to worry," Jessica explained smoothly. "Millie here will take photos of each horse so Alan can find the standouts. Additionally I'll be taking notes."

"Sounds like you girls are a well oiled machine," he remarked. "Wait here and I'll get your first horse."

Jessica watched him disappear into the barn before speaking in a low tone. "Use your phone to take pictures when he stands the horses up. Just try to act like you know what you're doing. I'll take notes and pedigrees. Got it?"

Millie offered a sharp nod as the barn door opened with a creak. Riley walked next to a leggy chestnut colt with two tall hind stockings. Millie admired his stretchy frame and loose walk as he moved past them. At the end of the driveway, Riley turned the colt around and walked back to them before standing the colt up for their inspection. Millie crouched slightly and lifted her cell phone to eye level, trying to find the best angle to photograph from. She worked around the colt, taking pictures from all sides while Jessica alternated between squinting intently and scribbling furiously in her notebook.

The process repeated itself several times. Millie felt a growing sense of appreciation for the differences in each of the young horses. Some were tall and light, others stocky and close coupled. A strong colt seemed to cower in fear, snorting at a rustle of the wind, while a small bay filly marched on determinedly.

After the last horse, Millie breathed a huge sigh of relief. "That was cool," she muttered to Jessica under her breath. "Kind of like a horse runway show,"

Jessica hunched over in laughter "I've never heard that one!"

Riley strode out of the barn, an empty lead shank in hand. "Well, that's the last of them. I'm sure Alan knows where to find me if he has any questions."

"Thank you Mr. McConnell," Jessica replied graciously. "You have some lovely stock."

"Do you girls do this often for Alan? I don't think I've seen you around the sales before."

Jessica fidgeted nervously. "Erm… Just part time. We usually work with Willowmere."

"Ah," he replied carefully. "Yes, I know Willowmere. The Jennings' have it now, eh? My family used to own that farm."

"Really?" Millie exclaimed, intrigued. "Can you tell me anything about the history?"

"It was a long time ago," Riley replied curtly. "My great grandfather bought the land and built the three original barns and manager's house. He passed it onto his son, who then passed it onto my uncle. I can't tell you about anything after that because it was sold many years ago. I understand the farm has changed quite a lot."

"It still has so much character though. Do you know what happened to the addition on the Yearling barns? The old map shows an extra room, but there's nothing there."

Riley shook his head. "Before my time, I'm afraid."

Jessica looked at Millie. "We should probably be going now before it gets late." She turned to Riley. "Thank you again. It was a pleasure."

Jessica called Alan once they were on the road back to Willowmere. "Millie took pictures, and I took notes," she explained. "I'll email it over to you tonight. There were a few that were nice, but the majority were quite plain. I don't think the mares Riley has out there are doing him any favors," she added.

"I really appreciate you girls doing this for me," Alan replied. "I didn't think he would have anything special in that group, but he's an old friend of mine and has had a rough go of it in this business."

"What do you mean?" Jessica inquired.

"He comes from a very successful family in the Thoroughbred industry. I don't know what his immediate family situation was, but I know he spent a lot of time at Willowmere growing up. His uncle, John McConnell, owned it back then after inheriting it from his father.

"When his uncle died unexpectedly, there was a big dispute about what would happen to the farm and mares. There was an old will, directing that the farm and mares were to be auctioned off. Riley tried to protest it as much as he could, but he was just a college age kid and had no money for a lawyer.

"The few times I've heard him speak of it, he's maintained that there was another updated will, and that the farm was meant to be his. What I think killed him was not just losing the farm, but the horses. They had mares there with three or four generations of his family's breeding. All gone."

"Wow," Jessica murmured. "I had no idea. What did he do then?"

"I think he left Kentucky after that and tried his hand at several different things—exercise riding, training, managing. We were friends in our late teens, but didn't keep in close contact after he lost the farm. I know he spent some time in New York and Pennsylvania running smaller farms. He showed back up in town maybe five or ten years ago and bought the place he's at now. He got some cheap mares and I think is trying to work his way back up to having an elite program. It's an uphill climb though when your mares are average. I always go look at his stock because I'm rooting for him to get something special one of these days. It just hasn't happened yet."

"Are you close with him now?" Millie asked.

"I don't go out of my way to spend time with him, but I've known him for ages. He's a good guy, but he can be a bit bitter to spend time with. Feels like life chewed him up and spit him out, you know?"

"It sounds like he's had a hard life," Jessica said.

"He has," Alan agreed. "I hope for his sake he's able to do well for himself and move on from everything that was lost at Willowmere.

"Anyways," he cleared his throat. "I have to get going. But send me those notes. And thank you girls for everything, I hope we'll see each other soon."

After Alan ended the call, Millie and Jessica looked at each other, a heavy silence hanging over the car. "You don't think after all these years, Riley could still be hung up on Willowmere, do you?"

Jessica shook her head. "I really don't know Millie. If you're asking if he's behind the weird stuff at the farm, I just can't imagine that. He has his own farm to run, and he's a relatively respected professional in the industry. There would be no good reason for him to do it."

Millie nodded. "I just had to ask."

Jessica dropped Millie back at the house while she went to run some errands in town. She was glad to have some time to herself and think about what had transpired earlier that day.

She curled up on the couch under a blanket with a book and cup of tea. Just as she settled in, there was a knock at the front door. Millie groaned in frustration. "Coming," she hollered down the hall.

Joe stood at the door, toolbox in hand. "Jessica called a few minutes ago to say the washer broke again"

"Come in," Millie muttered. Butterflies swam in her stomach just being around him. She wished that Jessica would have warned her that he would be making an appearance.

"You been up to anything interesting today?" Joe asked, as he began disassembling something inside the washer.

"Nothing terribly exciting. Jessica took me out to lunch and I got to see a bit of Lexington, so that was cool. I've been here a week but otherwise haven't left the farm."

"You have to explore the area while you're here," he offered. "It's an incredible place. Where are you from again?"

"Vermont," Millie smiled. "Not nearly as many horses around there. And the winters are a lot colder."

"I bet," he nodded. "I'm from South Dakota. The first time I came here, I felt like I was in a different world. Horses everywhere, rolling hills."

"What are your favorite places to go here?" Millie asked.

"There are so many," he smiled. "About an hour from here, there's a historical Shaker Village estate with some great hiking, if you're into that. And the Kentucky Horse Park is amazing too."

"What about farm tours?" Millie asked. "I keep hearing about them, but are they worth it for people like us, who get to be around horses every day anyways?"

Joe nodded. "Definitely. Choose wisely, but most of the tours will take you to the stallion barns. You'll be able to get up close to Kentucky Derby winners and multi million dollar earning racehorses. They have a different energy about them, you know? It's hard to explain, but I would highly recommend doing at least one."

"I'll have to do that,"

"Actually," he replied thoughtfully. "Skyfront Farm is just up the road and has a new stallion who won the Breeders Cup Classic last fall. I have some friends there, I could probably get us a private tour if you wanted?"

"I would love that!" Millie said with enthusiasm. "If it isn't too much trouble, of course," she added hastily.

Joe grinned. "I think it would be fun. Let me call my buddy and I'll let you know when." He stood up and dusted his hands off. "In any case, hopefully your washer is fixed for the moment. Tell Jessica to call me if there are any more issues. And I will let you know when I hear back about our tour at Skyfront."

Jessica arrived back at the house several hours later. "Joe came and fixed the washer," Millie informed her.

Jessica smiled. "I'm so glad you two got to spend some time together getting to know each other."

Millie raised an eyebrow. "Excuse me? Did you deliberately call him out when I was alone here?"

Jessica snickered. "Maybe."

"What have I done to give you the impression that I want to spend time with Joe?" Millie implored, her voice exasperated. Though she had enjoyed their chat, she couldn't understand why Jessica would suddenly be playing matchmaker.

"Oh, nothing on your end, Millie. It's just that Joe has been moping around the maintenance building for the past six months since his ex-girlfriend dumped him for another guy.

You showing up here is the first thing he's seemed interested in since." Jessica explained with a wide smile.

"I don't think he's interested," Millie sputtered out. "He knows I'm just an intern. Probably feels bad for me being out here and not knowing anyone."

Jessica shrugged. "Not here for a long time, here for a good time?" she winked.

Millie laughed and threw a pillow at her. "You're crazy. He's just being nice to me."

Jessica snorted and crossed her arms. "Whatever, all I know is that when Chloe was hired four months ago, he didn't wander around to the barns asking the other grooms if she had a boyfriend."

"He did not ask you that!"

Jessica raised her hands and smiled. "Maybe. A girl never tells her secrets."

Millie rolled her eyes. "Has anyone ever told you how annoying you are?"

Jessica beamed. "Many times!"

The next morning dawned warm and humid, with dark, threatening clouds. "Will the pregnant mares still get turned out today?" Millie asked Jessica with concern. "The weather report said there is going to be a pretty big storm later this morning."

Jessica nodded. "I'm guessing they'll go out, unless we get tornado warnings or something. Even then, in a lot of cases, the horses are safer outside than locked in the barn, in case the roof collapses."

"But Kentucky doesn't get tornadoes, right?"

"Not usually, but it has happened. A few years ago, a big one wiped out a town on the other side of the state."

"Good to know," she replied, regretting that she asked.

They drove in silence to the foaling barn, the dark sky looming ominously ahead.

"Sloane's back," Millie observed as they pulled up to the front doors of the barn.

Jessica glanced at Millie with sympathy. "She got back yesterday, and I hear she's been on a bit of a cleaning rampage. Good luck today."

"Hopefully I won't need it!"

Millie walked into the barn with purpose, stopping to look over the large whiteboard listing which mares had foaled. "Good morning!" she greeted Sloane, in her most chipper voice. "I see we've had some new arrivals?"

Sloane gave a curt nod. "Wonderstruck went last night, so Dr. Wells will be out this morning to check over the filly. Bella Notte foaled yesterday afternoon, but the filly had broken ribs, so they are on stall rest for a week."

"Is that normal?" Millie inquired. "Why would a foal have broken ribs?"

"Not many foals get them, but it's not rare. Sometimes during foaling they'll get squeezed too tight. We don't even X-ray them usually, you can tell just by feeling their rib cage. A little hairline fracture will resolve itself within a week or two of stall rest, but it can be really serious if they go outside and run around with it.

"It's one of those things that people who don't regularly deal with foals wouldn't think about. Aside from blood tests to make sure the foal is healthy, rib checks are one of the most important reasons to have a vet check over the foal before they're turned out for the first time."

The girls walked together to the double sized foaling stall.

Wonderstruck's broad, white marked face glanced at them with mild surprise. The foal, sensing her dam's reaction, leapt to her feet, her hooves slipping precariously in the straw. "Oh wow!" Millie exclaimed as the filly stood upright, her legs shaking with exertion. Dark brown with just a small star marking her forehead, at just a few hours old, her chest was broad and powerful, with long, thick legs. "I think that's the biggest newborn I've ever seen."

Sloane offered a rare smile. "Well, she's definitely not the biggest foal we've ever had here. A strong filly for sure though. It will be interesting to see how much she weighs. What's your guess?"

"I guess I'm not really sure," Millie admitted. "How much could a foal weigh? 75 pounds?"

Sloane laughed. "So, if a Thoroughbred foal is born too much under 100 pounds, they're probably a little premature, or born sick. Every now and again, we'll get one that's around 90 pounds, but for us, the average weight is probably between 110 and 135. One like this, I'd guess around 150."

"Okay," Millie nodded. "My official guess in this imaginary contest is 146 pounds."

"My guess is 153," Sloane offered. "Let's go look at the old foaling cards before we turn out and we'll see what her previous foals were. I know Wonderstruck has had some big ones."

Millie trailed behind as Sloane made her way into the tack room, reaching into the high cabinets to grab a small black box. She flipped the lid open, revealing a colorful collection of note cards. "Lets see here," Sloane muttered under her breath as she thumbed through the cards. The corners of her mouth frowned, her hands growing more frantic. She spun around to face Millie, her eyebrows drawn together. "Is this something you did to entertain yourself on night watch? Is this funny to you?"

"What? What's wrong?" Millie inquired, perplexed.

Sloane shook her head, her mouth set and angry. "This!" she spit out, gesturing at the foaling cards. "Swapping out this year's information cards for old cards belonging to dead mares! You think it's funny to mess with me like this?

Millie blinked in surprise. "Sloane," she began earnestly. "I have no idea about this. I didn't even know you kept the foaling cards up there. Now, are you *certain* that this is the right box and not just, I don't know, a box of the old ones?"

Sloane silently held the box out for her to read. **IMPORTANT: Current year foaling cards (breeding dates, foaling history).**

"I mean, we keep back ups of all this information," Sloane explained, her voice shaking. "So it's not all lost. But I will have to go through and remake and organize the cards. Just... *why?*"

Millie took a deep breath. "Sloane... I think something strange is going on at this farm. And I'd like to find out why. Can you think of anyone who would want to see this farm shut down?"

Sloane's face hardened. "I really can't, Millie. A little advice from one girl to another though, you watch yourself out here. The Kentucky Thoroughbred community is a good ol' boys club, and they don't take kindly to strangers. I'll keep an ear out for you, but I wouldn't hold my breath." Glancing out the window at the rising sun, she turned away from the counter top and stalked her way out into the barn aisle. "Time to get these mares turned out for the day."

Millie was about halfway through mucking out the foaling barn, when she heard the rattling of the maintenance truck pulling up to the front doors. She set aside her pitchfork and walked out, to see Joe in the driver's seat with the window rolled down. "Hey," he smiled. "I just got off the phone with my buddy from Skyfront."

"And?" Millie asked eagerly.

"How does this evening sound after work? The grooms will be gone but he said there should be someone up at the barn watching the stallions who can pull them out for us."

Millie smiled. "That sounds really nice. How far is it from here?"

"Only about fifteen minutes, just on the other side of Fayette county. You can ride up with me, if you like. We can take the scenic route, it's a nice drive."

Okay," Millie agreed. "That would be great since I don't have my own car out here. If you don't mind, of course."

"Not at all." He stared at Millie for a long moment, before shifting the truck into reverse. "I guess I'll see you later then, Millie."

Chapter 11

"I heard someone's got a big date," Jessica sang as Millie stepped into the car."

Millie groaned loudly. "Jessica, it's not a date. We're just going up to look at some stallions. He's being a nice co-worker."

"Uh huh," Jessica replied, unconvinced.

"How did you hear about it, anyways?" Millie demanded. "I didn't tell anyone that I was going out with my *friend* tonight."

Jessica cackled loudly. "Maybe you didn't, but Joe sure did. He couldn't contain his excitement, told the older maintenance guy, Terry. From there I think it spread like wildfire."

"It's not a date," she reiterated.

"Not a date, got it. It sure doesn't hurt though when 'not dates' are with really cute, funny, kind guys who are super into you, does it?"

Millie shook her head and buried her face in her hands. "I can't deal with you," she laughed as she got out of the car.

Once inside, she had just enough time to put on a clean shirt and hurriedly run a brush through her tangled hair before the doorbell rang. Joe stood on the doorstep, a crooked grin on his face as Jessica held the door. "Millie's not even ready yet, come inside, please"

Millie turned the corner and smoothly cut her off. "I'm actually ready now. We should be on our way, right Joe?"

He nodded. Millie stepped out onto the porch and glanced back at Jessica. "I shouldn't be late, I'll text you if something changes. Bye bye!"

Once they were in Joe's pickup truck, he burst out laughing. "What was that about?"

Millie rolled her eyes. "Apparently word on the street was that we have a hot date. She was foaming at the mouth for details earlier! I don't think she'll let me go to sleep tonight without hearing every detail."

Joe wiggled his eyebrows. "So that's what this is? A hot date?"

"Not you too!"

There was an easy silence on the drive to Skyfront Farm. Joe was right—the view from the passenger seat was breathtaking. Rolling green pastures were plentiful, accented by imposing barns, dark fences, and freshly bloomed flowering trees. Foals grazed next to watchful mothers, the lowering sun framing everything in a soft orange filter.

Joe turned down the radio and glanced over at her. "I don't think I've asked you, what kind of music are you into?"

Millie shrugged. "I'm not picky, but I usually find myself turning on the soft rock station. You?"

"Heavy metal, it's all I listen to," he deadpanned.

Millie snickered and reached across the center console to punch him in the arm. "Tell me the truth!"

"Why do you think I'm lying?" he teased. "You barely know me."

"That's true," she considered. "But I've long been a believer in first impressions, and I think I'm a pretty good judge of character."

At the red light, he glanced over and held her gaze. "So Millie Wright, what was your first impression of me? So I can tell you if you were right about me."

Millie laughed nervously. "Only if you tell what *your* first impression of me was. Deal?"

He smirked. "Sure."

"Okay," she cleared her throat. "I thought you seemed like, you know, a straight shooter. Nice guy. The sort who calls his mother on his day off, grew up with a nice family with lots of siblings. An outdoorsy type for sure, maybe a dog fan, a picture of his longtime girlfriend on his bedside table. You know, that type." There was a long, awkward pause. "...Which of course leads me to the ultimate conclusion that you would like country music, no pop."

Joe drew out a long whistle. "Wow. All that from a first impression?"

"People watching is kind of my thing," she explained apologetically. "How did I do?"

He laughed, grinning broadly. "I mean, a lot of that is subjective. But yeah, you actually got most of it right, except for one thing."

Millie felt heat rising up her neck. "Your turn!" she rushed out.

He glanced over at her, his expression impossible to read. "I thought you seemed like the most interesting person I had met in a really, really long time."

Millie felt like her stomach dropped to the pavement rushing beneath the car. Before she could sputter out a response, he cheerfully announced "Oh look, we're here!"

Skyfront Farm was orderly and imposing. By the tall, wrought iron gates, there was a guard shack with a bored looking man sitting inside. Joe rolled his window down. "Joe Danielson, Chuy Cortez said he would let you know we were coming?"

"Yeah, you'll head up to the first barn on your right." He abruptly closed the window, pressed a button and spun his chair around to face the small television set in the corner. The gates opened before them and Joe slowly drove through.

"He seems really enthusiastic about his job, doesn't he?" Millie inquired.

"Absolutely. Employee of the month material for sure."

Millie bit her lip with worry as a thought crossed her mind. She felt as if the JMD lighter was burning a hole through the pocket on her jeans. "What's your middle name?" she asked, trying to sound casual.

He raised an eyebrow at her. "Running a background check on me? There's nothing but a speeding ticket on me, but have at it."

"No, no, of course not," Millie laughed nervously. "I was just curious. I like to know a person's full name."

Joe shrugged. "Matthew. Not a very exciting name I'm afraid."

Millie's face remained unchanged, but inwardly her stomach felt sour. Joseph Matthew Danielson—JMD. It had to be Joe's lighter. But what would he have to gain from sabotaging the farm? Millie tried her best to push the thoughts away as they approached the ornate stallion barn.

The rich oak walls gleamed with good care, the brass name-plates all freshly polished. Millie couldn't believe a barn could be so immaculate as Joe and her stood in the doorway of the barn. A short man came out of what appeared to be the office. "Joe, man, it's good to see you. How've you been? And who's your friend?"

"Millie, she's the new intern over at Willowmere. Millie, this is Chuy—he's the stallion foreman here."

"Nice to meet you," Millie said, pasting a smile on her face, though her mind was miles away.

"You like working at Willowmere, Millie? I hear you guys have been having a rough season." Chuy said, shaking his head. "We all have them, but it doesn't make it any easier."

Millie grimaced. "It's a beautiful farm, and I've only been there a week. It's been an experience for sure."

Joe laughed. "What, you didn't think solo night watch was part of the job description?"

Millie snorted. "It was more the whole 'night watch quitting because of a haunted radio' that told me things are a little different out there."

Chuy chuckled. "A haunted radio? That's a new one, even for me."

Millie shook her head. "Trust me, that's barely the beginning of it all!"

Chuy smiled. "Well, if you ever get tired of the ghosts, we always need help around here. Let me show you guys around—this is, of course, our stallion barn."

He led them deeper into the barn. "It seems so serene here," Millie remarked. "I expected everything to feel more anxious somehow, since the stallions live here."

Chuy nodded. "You're not wrong, Millie—stallions can have a lot of nervous energy and be quite destructive. What I've found is that they appreciate a solid routine. Every night they come back to their stalls for some quiet time, where we leave them alone. We try to keep each day as similar as possible and match each stallion up with their own groom so they can build a rapport."

He paused by the first stall and slid open the door. "This is Indigo Warrior. He won the Breeders Cup Sprint two years ago. His first foals are hitting the ground now and we're really liking them so far."

Millie smiled as the dark stallion stretched his nose out the door. She reached to scratch his forelock, laughing as he gently nipped at her arm before she pushed him back in. They continued around the block of stalls, admiring each horse. Some were tall and lanky, others, like Indigo Warrior, were stocky and powerful looking.

"All the stallions here were accomplished race horses, we only breed the best. Of course, some are more well known than others. This last one here is the one I'm most excited to show you. In here," he began, gesturing to a tall wooden door. "Is Taking Flight. Last year's Breeders Cup Classic winner by a record fifteen lengths. This is his first year standing at stud. He's been a little... challenging to figure out."

Chuy unlatched the door and slowly opened it, Millie and Joe carefully trying to peer through the crack in the door as he entered. "Hey boy, easy now," Chuy murmured as he clipped a shank to his halter. The stallion snorted, his teeth making a distinct clacking sound as he lunged at the air. Millie and Joe's eyes met, their eyebrows raised.

The door slid open and Taking Flight stepped through, his neck arched, eyes flitting around nervously. "Wow..." Millie trailed off as he marched into the center aisle, Chuy looking like a rag doll attached to the end of the lead shank.

"I guess I didn't realize how *big* he is," Joe noted.

"He's 17.2," Chuy huffed. "And he wants everyone to know that he's big man on campus here."

Millie stepped forward with caution. The stallion flicked an ear towards her, *probably sizing me up*, she thought wryly. Taking Flight was a masterpiece of a horse, there was no doubt. From his intelligent face, to the strong slope of his shoulder, clean legs, and powerful hind end, she could see why there was so much buzz surrounding the horse.

He shook his head and pawed at the air. "At the risk of sounding obtuse, what is wrong with him?" Millie inquired.

Chuy laughed. "It's a good question, one we've been trying to figure out. His trainer and grooms from the track say he was a model citizen. As soon as he came here, all that went away. We're hoping that part of this is just missing his old routine at the track. We have him in the stall with the solid door, so he can't look into the aisle, which seems to keep him calmer. We turn him out far away from the other stallions, but he just runs the fence line constantly."

"But wouldn't that make things worse, being all alone? Aren't horses herd animals?" Joe asked.

Chuy shrugged. "Horses are herd animals, but anytime he was in a paddock near another horse, he would threaten to run through the fence. Plus, the stallions here are too valuable to get beaten up by another horse."

Millie nodded in understanding. "I do understand. That seems like a sad life for a horse though."

"We're hoping he settles down so he can have a more normal life." Chuy sighed.

"Jeffrey, the security guy? You probably talked to him. His idea was to give Taking Flight his own pet goat! Could you imagine? He would kill it in seconds!"

"Jeffrey?" Millie wondered aloud, turning to Joe. "Wasn't there someone named Jeffrey working at Willowmere awhile

90

back?"

Joe looked thoughtful. "I think you may be right. That was just before my time there, so I wouldn't recognize him. It's not that uncommon of a name though."

"Actually, I'm pretty sure he said he came from Willowmere," Chuy confirmed. "He's kind of an odd character, I don't have to deal with him much."

"Small world I guess," Millie smiled as Chuy led Taking Flight back into his stall, wondering how she could talk to Jeffrey without it being suspicious.

As Chuy and Joe bantered back and forth, Millie felt distracted, shifting her feet impatiently. There was a key suspect just outside, and all they could talk about was the demise of the local churro stand! After what felt like an eternity, Joe glanced at Millie. "We should probably get going and let you finish up here."

Millie nodded, trying to temper her enthusiasm. "Thank you so much for giving us the grand tour," she graciously told Chuy. "It was amazing to see these guys up close."

"Anytime," Chuy nodded. "And let us know if you're ever in need of employment here in Kentucky," he offered with a wink.

Millie laughed and walked out into the warm spring evening, Joe trailing next to her.

Millie grabbed her seat belt and settled into the passenger seat of Joe's truck. "So," he began, glancing over at her as he turned the ignition. "Do you want to grab a bite to eat?"

Millie chewed her lower lip. She *did* want to spend more time with Joe. She liked his unassuming nature, the casual way his hand found her lower back. She worried about the lighter, fussed over the fear of missed opportunity to question Jeffrey the security guy.

Joe mistook her hesitation for rejection. "It's fine, it's getting late any—"

"I'd like that.," she cut him off. She reasoned that she couldn't talk to Jeffrey with Joe around anyways. Plus, she could ask Joe questions about himself without it being odd. Like, for instance, why he dropped a lighter in a foaling mare's stall earlier that week.

Joe said he knew of a hole in the wall barbecue place not far from where they were, so Millie rode along in companionable silence, trying to organize her thoughts. Joe didn't press her for mindless chatter, which she appreciated.

They sat down in a small corner booth, Joe looking a bit uncomfortable as he stared down at his menu. Millie didn't mean to be so quiet, she just couldn't get rid of the ringing in her head that she may be sitting across from a criminal. When she asked what he was getting, she knew her voice sounded entirely too high, but it was better than awkward silence.

After the waiter had taken their orders, Millie decided she had to get to the bottom of things. "Do you smoke?"

Joe looked quizzical. "Uh, no?" He snorted with laughter. "Where did that come from?"

Joe's laughter annoyed Millie. She reached in her pocket and threw the lighter on the table. "Does this look familiar to you?"

Joe carefully held it between his fingers, rolling it back and forth. "Where did you find this?"

"You tell me."

Joe sighed, rubbing his eyes. "I'm not sure where you found it, because I *lost* it. Last week, I got home from work and I didn't have it with me. Checked my car, kept an eye out around the farm, didn't find it. That's all I know."

Millie narrowed her eyes."Why do you carry a lighter if you don't smoke?"

Joe leaned back and crossed his arms. "If I answer that, do I get to ask you a question?"

"Fine," she relented.

"I carry a lighter for two reasons. First, because it belonged to my grandfather, John Michael Danielson, and has sentimental value. Second, because it's just a handy thing to carry considering I work in the maintenance department. Does that satisfy your curiosity?"

"Why was it in Dorothy's stall, with all that highly flammable straw bedding?"

He raised his eyebrows. "probably because I was in there fixing her stall light on Monday. Sloane told me it was out. I do agree, that's a dangerous place for it. I'll have to be more careful."

Millie pursed her lips. She hadn't *really* thought Joe was guilty of anything, and his excuses were logical. However, she had hoped her first interrogation would be a more fruitful endeavor. She grumbled in frustration and slid the lighter across the table to him. "Here. All yours."

Joe was grinning with amusement when the perky waitress placed a steaming plate of cheese fries between them. After she walked away, he leaned in conspiratorially. "So Sherlock, are you going to tell me what you're really up to?"

Millie was taken aback. "What do you mean?"

"You know, always asking questions, looking into things. I see you, Millie. And if you want to start a detective agency, I'm here for you. I don't think I'm smart enough to contribute, but I will support you in all your crime solving ventures."

Millie laughed shrilly. "I don't know what you're talking about."

"Give it up Millie," he told her, twirling his fry in the hot cheese. "I saw your eyes light up when 'Jeffrey' was mentioned. Are you going to go interrogate him too?"

Millie stared at her plate, unsure if she should try to deny it.

Joe's shoulders shook with laughter. "If you're going to do that, at least let me come. That guy must weigh, like, at least two-fifty. If he decided he doesn't like your questions, I'm not sure you'd be much of a match."

"Whatever," she replied, trying to hold onto her irritation, though the corner of her mouth twitched with amusement.

"Will you at least fill me in on the investigation? Do you have any suspects, other than myself of course?" he inquired teasingly.

Millie shook her head. "A good detective never gives up her secrets!"

"What was my motive anyways? I'm always curious to hear why people think I'm committing these heinous crimes."

"You know—" Millie paused, fork halfway to her mouth. "I hadn't really gotten that far in my investigation."

Millie had to hide her smile the whole drive home. The fading light cast shadows on the rolling green hills out the window. It was going to be a full moon soon.

The car slowed as they turned onto Old Mill Road, the sprawling black fence of Willowmere stretching up ahead. Millie glanced at the time on her phone. "Can you drive me into the farm and just drop me off at the foaling barn? It's a short walk back to the house."

"Did you forget something up there? I can wait to take you

back home, it's no big deal."

Millie shook her head. "No, I'll be fine. I could use some exercise anyways and it's a beautiful evening."

Joe wove the car down the narrow farm road leading to the foaling barn. "Is this because you want to talk to Connie?" he mused.

Millie raised her eyebrows and smirked. "Where would you get an idea like that?"

Joe stopped the car and looked over at her, his brown eyes searching hers. "Just please promise me that you'll be careful?"

"Of course," she whispered, her heart pounding as her eyes flicked down to his lips. "But," she began, clearing her throat. "If it really came down to it, I think I could take Connie on."

Joe snickered. "Whatever you say. Just do me a favor, and call me whenever you get it in your head to go 'question' Jeffrey. I can be your backup, or even the Holmes to your Sherlock."

"Really? You would come with me?"

Joe smiled in his crooked way, glancing over as he put the car back in drive. "I can't have you getting kidnapped or anything Ms. Wright. I'm growing quite fond of you."

He dropped her off by the front doors of the barn, with a quick wave as he pulled away. The night watch truck was parked, so Millie knew that Connie must be around. The mares whickered softly between mouthfuls of hay as she walked in. She pulled her jacket tighter around her shoulders, against the cool April wind blowing in from the far end.

"Hellooooo?" Millie called out.

"In here!" a voice distantly called out from the other end of the barn aisle.

Millie strode towards the voice, to find Connie inside a stall, crouched down in the deep straw under a mare. "Would you mind holding her? I've been trying to get a milk sample but she keeps walking off."

"Of course," Millie murmured, slipping into the stall and grabbing the mare's halter. *Lena Fever* the plate read. "Will she be the next one to foal?"

Connie shrugged her shoulders. "She's waxed and dripping milk, so she could go whenever. I just wanted to test it because I'm worried her colostrum is leaking out."

Millie followed wordlessly as Connie led her to the tack room and started digging through cabinets. "Ah, here we go," she muttered, pulling out a long black tube with a slanted silver end. Connie placed several drops of the milk she had collected on the slanted end, and pressed down with a glass plate, before pointing it to the ceiling and holding it up to her eye. "What is that?" Millie asked, fascinated.

"It's a refractometer," Connie explained. "It tells us how much colostrum is present in the milk. Right now, Lena is about at twenty-five, so her milk is still good. If she drops down too much, we know that we'll need to bottle feed colostrum to the foal from another mare."

"Is that why we keep colostrum containers in the freezer?" Millie asked.

"There are lots of times we might need it, including the mare leaking her milk prior to foaling, or in the case that she dies giving birth. You need to be prepared for anything when it comes to foaling."

Connie bustled around the room, cleaning the refractometer, writing things down in the record book. "Is there something I can help you with?" Connie asked, her back turned to Millie.

"I was actually wondering if I could ask you about some of the things you mentioned the other night. You know, when the power went out."

Connie's pen stilled over the record book. "I'm sorry Millie, but this isn't a good time."

"Can you at least tell me when all this started?" Millie pressed. "Look, I know something strange is going on at this farm, and *no one* will talk to me about it. I did night watch after you left, and I saw some things. Just please... tell me what you know."

Connie sighed. "I don't *know* anything, and I apologize for my outburst the other night. You have to understand, working twelve hour overnight shifts does something to a person. You're tired all the time, your body feels messed up from almost never seeing the sun."

"That does sound overwhelming," Millie admitted. "I was exhausted, and I only did it for a few nights. I can't even imagine when you've been doing it for months on end."

"Right," Connie nodded. "On the sixth straight night of this, you start questioning yourself. Like, did I already check the other side of the barn, or am I imagining it? Last week, I pulled out the hose to water, and all the buckets were already filled to the brim."

Millie felt her heart sink. "So, you think the strange things you mentioned were just a figment of your imagination?"

Connie shook her head and frowned. "It has to be. Sitting up alone at 2 AM, your mind will play tricks on you. Bucket clips spinning on their own, doors opening and closing themselves, items moving to the opposite end of the barn, the radio turning itself off and on—" She closed her eyes and inhaled sharply.

"You see Millie," she began with a gentle tone. "There is no explanation for it all. I got too tired, I had a few days off, and now everything is good. I'm trying to put it behind me. There's only about a month of foal watch left, then I'll have the option to move onto day shift."

Millie was skeptical, but sensed she was getting nowhere. "Okay," she nodded. "Understood. I'm going to head back to the house now, but if anything, and I mean *anything* happens, I want you to let me know."

Connie cocked her head and looked at Millie with an appraising gaze. "I didn't realize that 'private investigator' was in the spring intern job description now."

Millie rolled her eyes. "Not you too! I just have a curious mind is all!"

Millie heard the echoes of Connie's laughter as she walked down the tree lined drive away from the foaling barn. Under the setting sun, two foals played in a distant pasture, their mothers never far off. *What a perfect place*, she thought to herself, veering off the drive to follow the line of hedges that would lead her to Jessica's house. The narrow grass path wove between two pastures, but the horses kept their distance, raising their heads and snorting at the dark figure moving outside their space.

Her phone rang abruptly, ruining the tranquility of the evening. She swore under her breath, searching her pockets for her phone as the horses sprinted off to the other end of the pasture. "Hello?" she grumbled into the phone.

"Millie?" inquired the voice on the phone. "What's wrong with you?"

"Becca!" she laughed. "What are you doing calling from a random number? You're lucky I picked it up."

"It's the inn we're staying at in Ireland," Becca explained. "My phone screen cracked and it keeps glitching. Thankfully everything on my phone is saved to my computer, so I do have all my contact numbers. I wasn't sure I would remember how to dial a landline though."

"You're so dramatic," Millie teased. "So tell me, what's new on the Emerald Isle? You know, I'm expecting you and Callie to be able to perform a proper Irish jig for me when you get back."

"Oh my gosh, stop it. Callie dragged me to an Irish basket weaving class one of the first days we were here, and I said 'that's about as much culture as I can handle.'"

"But what if that was your calling in life? They say everyone has a secret talent, maybe that's yours."

"I'm pretty sure my secret talent is walking down quaint cobblestone streets, and hiking up to the Cliffs of Moher." Becca replied flatly.

"I'm so jealous," Millie moaned. "I want to see pictures of all of it. Everything. Even the hotel bathroom."

"Regretting your choice to shovel manure in the Horse Capital of the World yet?"

Millie was quiet for a long moment, glancing up at the darkening sky. She wasn't far from the house, but lingered outside, feeling a deep ache as she looked at the cozy cottage, warm light spilling from the windows. "No, I don't think I regret it. It's just different than I expected. And hard being away from Woodstock, and you guys of course."

Becca seemed to consider this. "That makes sense. But seriously, you must be learning so much. And it's good to meet new people—we grew up so sheltered in Woodstock. Sometimes it's easy to forget there's an entire world outside of that."

"For sure," Millie agreed. "Plus, if I had never come out here, I never would have learned about the legend of the Lockhurst Lady."

"Not this again!" Becca groaned. "Please tell me you're not crawling around some abandoned tunnel right now."

"Of course not. But tomorrow I'm going with Joe to interrogate one of the farm's old employees."

"Oh, so now Joe helps you interrogate people? Things are getting cozy," Becca teased.

"He's nice, and has good taste in barbecued food!" Millie defended herself.

"Sounds like your priorities are straight." She replied dryly. "How do you know about his taste in food?"

"Because we went to dinner tonight," Millie squeaked out.

"Millie! How could you keep this from me!"

"I'm telling you now!" she protested.

"Does Joe know about your passion for crime solving?"

"I think he's onto me," Millie admitted. "He seems to think it's really funny."

"Probably because it *is* kind of funny?"

"I've had enough of you, and I have to get up early tomorrow."

"Okay," Becca sighed into the phone. "Let's talk again soon, yeah? And I want you to be careful."

"I always am, you know that."

Chapter 12

"Y ou sure you're okay to ride in the trailer with her?" Stewart called out as he closed the back doors of the horse trailer.

"Of course," Millie replied with false confidence. She heard the truck start and swallowed her fears down. The floor began to move as she clutched the lead shank attached to Lena Fever. The blood bay mare's coat was dark with sweat and Millie dimly noticed how hot it was inside the trailer.

"Easy mare," she murmured as the mare lurched forward precariously, her eyes wide with fear. Millie jingled the lead shank. "Come on girl, you need to stay standing."

Lena blinked at her with glassy eyes, her nostrils flared red with exertion. Millie silently prayed that the mare didn't collapse on her in the moving trailer. She glanced behind the mare and saw only the blood soaking the shavings by her hind legs.

The scenery of Central Kentucky flashed through the trailer window. She grabbed the metal bar covering the window for balance as the trailer jolted over a bump in the road. Lena groaned again as her knees attempted to buckle, Millie's heart thudding as she shook her halter in an attempt to keep the mare standing.

The day had started normally enough, with Millie and Sloane checking the mares and giving medication before turning out. Millie always enjoyed the quiet rhythm of morning chores, checking in with each mare. When she had gotten to Lena Fever, the first thing she noticed was the steam billowing off her into the crisp morning air, her neck soaked with sweat.

A tense phone call to Stewart later, they dragged her into the foaling stall and awaited the arrival of her foal. And waited. Then waited some more.

When Stewart arrived, he slid an arm into her, checking the position of the foal. "Breech," he muttered. "The foal is trying to come out backwards, with its hind legs first." With a grim shake of the head and a phone call to the Jennings', it was decided that Lena was headed straight to the hospital.

"Someone's going to need to ride in the back with her to make sure she doesn't lay down and get stuck," Stewart called out as he jumped in the truck. Sloane disappeared into the tack room, leaving Millie to begrudgingly climb in with the thrashing mare.

The trailer slowed under her feet—another peek out the window confirmed they had made it. *Maxwell Equine Medical Center* was embossed on the stone pillars framing the front gate. *And not a moment too soon,* Millie grimaced as Lena stomped her front hoof, slamming her body into the side of the trailer.

Almost as soon as she felt the truck shift into park, she heard voices surrounding the trailer and the ramp dropped. The sudden brightness was disorienting. Millie felt like a child on ski's clutching to a rope tow on the bunny slope as the mare dragged her down the ramp into the sunlight. Millie would have thought that the pain and stress would subdue the freight train attached to her lead shank. Instead, Lena was blind with panic, lunging forward desperately with stilted steps.

Hospital staff in gowns and latex gloves surrounded them, urging the mare through a small doorway in a concrete block building. Inside was a large open room, the floor covered in black mats, walls padded with blue cushioning. A horse sized scale sat along the front wall, in the corner a counter top and cabinets near a set of stocks surrounded by expensive looking equipment.

The smell of antiseptic overwhelmed Millie's senses. They were guided to a bare stall, where Millie held onto the mare and tried to step out of everyone's way. A blonde technician checked her vitals while vets bustled around her hind end. "Hang on tight to her, don't let her step back now," someone instructed Millie "We're going to try to pull the foal out while she's standing, don't let her lay down."

She grabbed Lena's halter and held her head up as the mare tried to lean back, groaning in pain. From her head, she couldn't see what the vets were attempting, but she heard chains clinking and men pulling in an attempt to free the foal.

With every passing moment, Millie knew it became less likely that the foal would survive. Lena was exhausted, her neck lathered with white foam, her eyes glassy. *Please, please, please let them be okay*, she silently willed. Millie's heart pounded with adrenaline, but all she could do was comfort the mare.

For a minute, the only sounds were the grunts of the vets and technicians pulling the hind legs of the foal, and the heavy breathing of the mare. Finally, there was a loud *splosh* of fluid, "We got the hips out, and shoulders are coming along," a tech called out to Millie. "Just another minute hopefully."

With another solid push from the mare, the foal was released, someone reaching their arms out to break its fall.

Lena came alive again, raising her head and letting out a piercing whinny. Millie cringed, letting her spin around to face the unmoving foal.

Several people gathered around it, one holding an oxygen mask on its nose, another rubbing it with towels to try to coax it into life. A young technician held a stethoscope to its side. "It's faint, but it has a heartbeat," she confirmed.

"Come on now, take a breath," the vet grumbled. "Someone grab me the crash kit! Now!" he called out, technicians scrambling to retrieve the drugs.

Millie felt like a useless bystander as she watched the attempts to revive the foal, jingling the lead shank as Lena halfheartedly pawed her leg. "We got it!" the tech exclaimed as the foal began to writhe with life, flanks rising and falling rapidly. Millie released a breath she hadn't realized she was holding.

The vet stood and gestured to Stewart. "You should talk to the Jennings' and find out what they want to do here. This foal, if it survives, will have a very long road ahead of it. The lungs don't sound great, I would not be surprised if it came down with pneumonia. It appears to be fully developed, but will need round the clock care to help stand and nurse. If it's going to live, I think the only option is to leave them both here at the clinic and see how it develops."

Stewart nodded grimly, his face ashen with stress. "Is it a colt or filly?"

The technician rubbing the foal peeked under its tail, its front legs thrashing about. "Filly."

Stewart sighed, running a hand down his face. "I will call them. This is an expensive mare, and the stallion retired last year, so I think they'll opt to give it a shot."

"Just make sure they understand that we are not out of the

woods," the vet cautioned.

"She could very well pass on her own in the next 24 hours. They are welcome to call me with any questions as well."

"Of course," Stewart confirmed. "I'll go outside and call them now.

Once the foal seemed stable, they were moved into a stall, deeply bedded with golden straw. A technician took Lena from Millie, while a group of people rolled the foal onto a gurney to be carried. Stewart strode back in, slipping his phone back into his pocket. "Richard said to keep trying on the foal," he confirmed. "He said to give it 24 hours, and if there's no improvement we should talk about euthanasia."

The vet nodded in confirmation. "I think that's fair. We'll give you a call in the morning and let you know how things progress."

"I appreciate it. Such a pity, Lena Fever is one the best mares they have. Are you ready to go, Millie?"

Millie offered an affirmative nod before walking out into the daylight, towards the farm truck. "You can ride back to the farm in the trailer again if you like," Stewart joked.

Millie gave a thin smile. "Just that one trailer ride was quite enough for a lifetime, thanks for the offer though."

Stewart shook his head in dismay. "This is why I try to stick to yearlings these days. The breeding game is not for the faint of heart, you're always just a moment away from disaster it seems."

"Why were they talking about putting down that foal? Don't they want it to live?"

Stewart let out a heavy exhale. "When you're running a farm the size of Willowmere, you have to be considering the business side of things in every decision. *If* she survives, the hospital bill is going to be enormous, thousands and thousands of dollars spent on one foal. A weak, sick foal, probably won't become a strapping yearling that will sell for a profit for the farm. If it lives, they'll also have to pay the stallion fee so the foal can get registered. Again, more money for a horse that may never see a racetrack."

"I understand," Millie replied. "But I sure can't imagine having to make that decision. Do you think she will live?"

"I really don't know, Millie. She's in bad enough shape that it's possible she'll pass away tonight. She could also shock us and be standing and nursing tomorrow. I've seen it go both ways."

They drove the rest of the way in silence, the beautiful morning taken over by dark clouds and fat raindrops on the windshield.

Chapter 13

The rest of the day took on a heaviness that Millie couldn't quite shake as she went through the motions. Her mind kept flitting back to Lena Fever and her bright bay filly. At the end of the day she asked Stewart for an update, but he hadn't heard anything. Though she wasn't sure if she was imagining it, it seemed a hush had descended over the farm. The steady background noise of tractors and vets and cars had disappeared, leaving only the steady drumming of rain on the roof.

Sloane sent her down to the maintenance shop to get more disinfectant. On the drive past the yearling filly field, she saw the small, fluffy calico cat sprinting towards its hollow tree house and shook her head. *What a strange place.*

Spotting Chloe walking into the tack room, she stopped the golf cart at the barn. "Hey there," she called out. "It's been awhile since I've seen you."

The blonde girl pursed her lips in irritation. "Well, here I am."

Millie paused, frowning at Chloe's attitude. "Is everything okay?" she asked carefully.

"I don't know. You tell me."

"You're going to have to be more specific," Millie countered.

"Are we talking about the mare that was rushed to the clinic this morning? The weather? The weird things that won't stop happening?"

"The latter," she replied dryly. "I don't *get* you," she spit out with anger. "Why are you running around making this stuff up?"

Millie was taken aback. "Excuse me? Making what up?"

Chloe rolled her eyes. "Give it up, Wright. You've been going around telling ghost stories like you're at summer camp. What I can't figure out is *why*? Things were just fine right up until you showed up."

"You call Mr. Jennings getting run over by a stampede of loose yearling colts okay?" she asked in disbelief. "And I'll add, I never *asked* to fill in for night watch. It happened because Connie got scared off in the middle of the night. You can't blame me for that."

"Whatever," Chloe replied, spinning around. "Just know that I'm onto you," she called over her shoulder, leaving Millie reeling in the aisle.

In the early morning drama, Millie had almost entirely forgotten about going to question the security guard at Skyfront Farm. She had to cover up her confusion when Joe stopped by in the afternoon to confirm.

He picked her up promptly after work, Millie watching for his truck from the front door so he wouldn't have time to walk to the house. She hollered to Jessica that she would be back later, but didn't offer further explanation. She was in a weird mood and didn't have the energy to explain where she was going.

Joe turned down the radio and glanced over at her "Do you have a plan?"

108

"A plan?" she echoed back.

"Yeah, like, do you know what you're going to say to Jeffrey?" he asked.

Millie shrugged. "Not really, but now that you mention it, I think I might just go straight for the kill. 'Jeffrey, have you been deliberately sabotaging Willowmere Farm? I have the police on speed dial, by the way.'"

Joe looked uneasy. "Millie, what if he *is* behind some of the stuff? I think you need to have at least some cover story."

"Okay," she contemplated. "What do you suggest then?"

"I'm coming up blank, detective."

"Unhelpful," she interjected. "How about I try sticking as close to the truth as I can? Tell him I'm an intern, that I've been doing research on the farm and the graveyard, and want to know if he has any stories or information on the alleged hauntings?"

Joe laughed. "That sounds ridiculous. But sure, and I can stay in the background as your silent bodyguard, only there to ensure you don't get kidnapped for your intrusive questions."

Millie punched him in the arm. "Deal."

When they pulled up to the guard shack, Jeffrey was inside. His back was turned to the window, facing a computer screen with headphones on. "Looks like he's occupied Millie, we should come back another time." Joe said with sarcasm, reaching his arm out the window to press the red assistance key.

Jeffrey jumped at the sound of the buzzer, spinning around to face them. Looking puzzled, he raised a hand in greeting and pressed a button to open the front gate before turning back around.

Millie giggled. "I think we've been dismissed."

Joe shook his head. "No wonder Chuy practically was

foaming at the mouth to hire you."

Millie snorted and unbuckled her seat belt. "Whatever you say. Let's go talk to him."

Together they walked up to the door of the guard shack. Joe rapped on the door. Jeffrey stood and turned around, placing his headphones around his neck. "Yeah?"

"Sorry to bother you," Millie began smoothly. "You must be Jeffrey?"

He looked at her appraisingly, his eyes dragging over her before flitting to Joe. "Depends on who's asking."

"I'm so sorry, where have my manners gone!" Millie exclaimed, sticking her hand out.

"I'm Millie Wright. And this is Joe," gesturing next to her. "I'm an intern at Willowmere. When we were here yesterday to see the stallions, Chuy mentioned that you used to work there?"

"I did, a few years ago," he replied, his expression guarded. "So did a lot of other people though. That farm changes staff like I change my underwear."

"Did you ever visit the graveyard when you were there?" she inquired.

"Of course, everyone did. Not much to see, but it's a cool spot."

"So you never saw anything strange while you were there? Because Stewart thought that you had."

"Stewart knows nothing," he spit out. "And I need to get back to my job."

Millie held a hand on the door he was trying to close. She felt Joe shift unsteadily behind her. "I'm doing research on some of the old legends of the farm. It has quite a history, as I'm sure you know. I was hoping to speak with people who have had personal experience with the... *oddities* of the farm."

"I don't know what you're talking about," he said, avoiding eye contact.

"Jeffrey," she began. "I believe you. I've seen things too."

Jeffrey let out a long exhale. "What have you seen?"

"Personal items moving themselves around. Lights, radios, water spigots, turning themselves off and on. Maybe a ghost. You know, normal stuff." Millie paused for a moment. "Also, a calico cat living inside a tree," she added as an afterthought.

Jeffrey laughed. "They thought I was crazy, or a drunk. But you've seen it too, yeah?"

Millie snickered. "I thought I was losing it when I saw the ghost."

He nodded. "The Lockhurst Lady."

"I know. When was the first time you saw her?"

"I only saw her once, when I first started working there. About four years ago."

"Did you follow her?"

He laughed. "Are you kidding me? I was glued to the spot. I had—*have*—zero interest in being a ghost hunter."

"So you don't know what the deal with the cat is?" she asked, disappointed.

He shook his head. "I think I saw it a few times around the Yearling Barn, but I never got close to it."

"I think whatever, or whoever, the Lockhurst Lady is, takes care of it." Millie confided. "I followed it out to the hollow tree it lives in, and there were food and water dishes."

Jeffrey looked taken aback. "So, if it's taking care of a cat, you don't think it's a ghost?"

Millie shrugged her shoulders. "I guess that's the million dollar question, isn't it?"

"You're not going to tell the Jennings' that you talked to me, are you?" he asked nervously. "I didn't leave there on the best of terms."

"I can keep this between us if you prefer. All I care about is getting to the bottom of this."

Jeffrey raised his eyebrows in surprise. "Some intern you are... how long have you been there?"

"About a week," she replied curtly.

Jeffrey laughed. "Did the Jennings' put you up to this? Are you telling me you've seen all that in just a few days?"

"No, the Jennings' have no clue." Her voice took on a serious tone. "I think things have gotten worse. In the time I've been there, we've had staff injuries, horses loose, things damaged. I'm not looking to stir up trouble, but I can't help but wonder what's going on."

"I wish I could be of more help. It does sound like things have changed. It used to be a joke, that if you worked night watch long enough, you'd eventually see a ghost. Every weird thing I saw was spread out over a two year span, and it was never anything serious. Just bizarre little things, like one shoe would go missing, or your stuff would end up in a completely different place than you put it. It was always when I knew I was alone on the farm."

"I really appreciate you taking the time to talk with me,"

Jeffrey nodded and turned back to his computer, Millie watching the door slam in her face.

Millie was bursting at the seams with excitement when they got back in the car. "Did you hear that? It totally narrows down my suspect list if this has been going on for over four years. Chloe and Jessica have both only been there for less than a year. So I guess that leaves Stewart and Sloane?"

Joe looked at her in disbelief. "Have you considered that everything Jeffrey just told you could be a complete lie?"

Millie was taken aback. "Why would he lie? He works somewhere else now."

"Stewart implied he left under bad circumstances. Maybe he wants to get back at them now for firing him."

"I suppose it's possible," Millie admitted. "I'm not sure what he would have to gain from that though."

"Why do criminals do anything?" Joe countered. "You can't apply logic where there is none."

"I disagree with that. Revenge is a solid motive." she hesitated. "Maybe that's just because I'm a Scorpio though,"

Joe laughed. "Sure, blame your psychopathic nature on your star sign." He became somber and looked over at her. "I hate that you told him you knew about the cat. If he's behind that, he's going to be looking out for you snooping around. I think you should at least be carrying pepper spray, Millie."

"I know," she admitted. "I'm not totally dense though. I told him about the cat, but I didn't mention the tunnel."

"Tunnel?! What tunnel, Millie?" he asked, hitting the brakes.

"I guess I haven't mentioned those to you yet," she laughed. "Remember, until about 24 hours ago, I thought you might be the one doing all this."

Joe rolled his eyes. "Please tell me you're not planning to explore the tunnel?"

"Oh, I already did," Millie replied in a chipper tone. "Very interesting stuff. Also very dusty."

Joe dragged a hand down his face. "Where did you find it? And where did it go?"

"It was inside a hollow oak in the yearling filly pasture, where that cat lives. There's a trapdoor you can go down. It took me maybe fifteen minutes, but it eventually led to a crawl space under the Jennings' house."

"Do the Jennings' know about it?"

"I'm not sure. I considered calling to tell them, but honestly I'm a little worried they would be upset that I ended up in their house. Which of course, I didn't know was theirs until I looked out the window, but still."

Joe nodded, looking distant. "Why would there be a tunnel on the farm in the first place?"

"Certainly not for convenience sake," Millie added. "Between the trapdoor, and then crawling on my knees in the crawlspace to get to the basement, it was a dirty job."

Joe laughed. "Serves you right for being so curious."

"I think I need to find out more about the history of the farm, but I'm not sure where to start."

"You could try the library at Oaklyn Racecourse," Joe offered. "I don't know about this particular farm, but they keep lots of historical records of farms and events in the Lexington area."

Millie sighed. "Well, I guess I know where I'm headed tomorrow."

Millie sat on her bed, surrounded by notes when her phone rang. She glanced at the caller ID and felt a deep ache in her chest. "Hey Mom."

"Millicent. How have you been? You haven't been keeping in touch."

"I'm good," Millie replied, unsure of how much to divulge.

"Have you been able to spend much time with Kelly and Richard yet?"

"Actually," Millie cringed. "I still haven't met them. They've been tied up at the state hospital. Stewart, their yearling manager, has been left in charge of the farm. I've been mostly working in the Foaling Barn."

"In the hospital?" her mother zeroed in. "For what? I hope nothing serious?"

"Apparently the night before I got here, some colts got loose. When they were trying to catch him, Richard got trampled. I don't think he's critical at this point, but his injuries were bad enough the hospital wanted to keep him. Stewart told Kelly not to worry about the farm, so she hasn't left his side."

"Are you sure this is a good time to be interning there? It sounds like there's a lot going on," her mother asked worriedly.

"It's fine, Mother. Actually, I think they really need the help. They had a night watchman walk off the job last week, so I filled in a few nights, though I'm back on days now."

"You worked the graveyard shift?" her mother asked in disbelief. "Are you even learning anything or are you just a grunt? I knew I should have put my foot down and sent you to Ireland with the girls, especially after all the drama with your fath—"

Millie cut her off. "It's fine, Mom. Really. Everyone has been nice, and the farm is so beautiful."

There was a moment of silence on the phone. "Just as long as you're happy, I suppose," her mother sniffed.

"I am," Millie reassured her, biting her lower lip. "Have you heard anything from Dad?"

"He called from his first rest stop yesterday. He's heading into the One Hundred Mile Wilderness section of the trail, so I don't expect to hear from him again for a while," she replied stiffly.

"Did he seem okay?" She was desperate for any crumbs of news about her father, but knew better than to pry.

"He seemed well. Mentioned he got a postcard from you."

"Oh good," she replied, noting that her voice sounded hollow. "I was worried he wouldn't get it in time."

"Well then," her mother announced after an awkward pause. "I suppose I should let you go. And please don't be a stranger, will you?"

"I'll call you on Monday," she promised. "Love you, Mom."

"I love you too, dear."

Chapter 14

"What on earth..." Jessica trailed off as her jeep crept up Willowmere's main farm road. Ahead was a line of motionless cars. She shifted the car into park and opened her door. "We better go find out what's going on."

Millie felt an unease in her stomach walking along the tree lined drive. As the girls rounded the bend, Terry waved them over. "Good morning, ladies. Looks like we're going to have to use the back entrance today."

At his feet lay an enormous fallen oak tree. "Oh my gosh," Millie said. "What happened? It didn't even storm last night."

Joe silently gestured to her. He led her to the trunk of the tree. He glanced around, keeping his voice low. "It was cut down, Millie. This was deliberate."

Her eyes widened in disbelief. "Don't tell the others if you don't have to," she told him. "If Stewart won't do it, we need to contact the Jennings'."

He nodded grimly. "I put a call into Stewart and told him. He hasn't been out to look yet."

"Okay. We'll get everyone turned around and headed to the back entrance." She paused, glancing at the enormous tree. "I'd say you'll be spending some quality time with a chainsaw and tractor today."

Joe barked out an unamused laugh. "Not what I was planning when I started my day, but here we are."

Millie turned to walk away, glancing back to throw him a rueful smile. "Okay," she cleared her throat. "Let's get turned around here so we can take care of these horses," she said to Jessica, interrupting her conversation with Terry.

Jessica nodded. "We'll head up there now. Too bad we don't have a pair of shears, I don't think that gate has been used in years. I bet the overgrowth is terrible."

Jessica carefully backed her car down the narrow winding road before turning back onto Old Mill Road. "I didn't even realize there was a back entrance," Millie commented.

"We hardly ever use it. The only other time I can remember was when the front gate lost power last winter. We practically had to dig it out of a foot of ice then."

At the end of Old Mill, Jessica made a right turn onto Sinai Road. "It's right along here," she explained. "I think this entrance used to be for a house within the farm, but it's long gone now."

While the main entrance was sleek and imposing, this drive could have led to the Fayette County dump. The gravel drive was unmarked, the fence running along it old and rotting. Long fallen fence boards sat on the ground, the trees untrimmed and wild. A modest black cow gate hung across the drive. "Hop out," Jessica gestured. "No fancy electric gate out here, you'll have to open and close it by hand."

Millie grabbed onto the gate, pulling it across the dusty gravel, when she noticed fresh marks in the dust from the gate dragging. A quick glance at the hinges, showed cut vines carelessly tossed next to it. Someone had used this gate recently—to avoid detection?

She held the gate as the line of cars drove through, Jessica pulling over to wait for Millie. "Does maintenance work on this part of the farm?" she asked Jessica.

"You can ask Joe. I don't know if they're technically supposed to, but I'd reckon most of the time they're too busy dealing with the parts of the farm that we actually use and people see, to worry much about this end, aside from the occasional mow."

Overgrown hedges slapped the side of the car as they wound through the backside of the farm. On the right was a dilapidated tool shed, a small pile of rubble laying about seventy five feet away from it. "I think that's where the old assistant's cottage was."

"Do you know when it burnt down?" Millie asked, frowning as the gravel changed to pavement.

"No clue." Jessica let out a sigh as the view gave way to horses grazing in open fields, the farm once again appearing lush and manicured. "It's a shame that little bit of land is going to waste though. It's like another universe back there."

"I'm surprised they don't use it for something. I'm sure they could at least put employee housing or rentals there." Millie remarked.

"Yeah, but they would have to clear the land and build a house, which costs money. It costs nothing to let the land sit while they have no use for it," Jessica countered, glancing in her rear view mirror as she pulled up in front of the foaling barn. "Oh shoot," she grimaced. "Get out of the car fast so I can drive away before Stewart tries to talk to me."

Millie laughed. "Why are you avoiding Stewart?"

"Well, I can't imagine he's in a great mood today. Hopefully

119

for your sake he'll go easy on you because you're an intern!"

Millie rolled her eyes. "You're a real pain. I'll talk to you later."

"Have a great day now!" she grinned as she pulled away waving.

Millie steeled herself as Stewart's truck pulled up next to her. "Good morning," she sang, hoping her enthusiasm would deter any bad vibes.

"Millie. Did you see the tree?"

"I did," she replied cautiously.

He ran a hand through his hair in frustration. "I just don't get it," he spit out. "*Why* would somebody cut down a tree in the driveway? If someone had it out for the Jennings', wouldn't they burn the place to the ground or something?"

"Unless," Millie began with a level gaze, "Someone just wants them *off* the farm, not to destroy it."

"That doesn't make sense," he shook his head. "What good is an empty farm?"

"Maybe someone wants to buy them out."

Stewart cleared his throat. "In any case, I'm going to call the Jennings' shortly. They should be home in a day or two anyways, I'd rather not have them be totally shocked by the state or disarray at this farm."

"I think that's a good decision." she offered, silently relieved that she wouldn't have to call them herself.

"Millie?"

"Yeah?"

"I know you've been keeping your eyes open. But, if you get a chance, could you, uh… let your eyes wander a bit today? Just to see what they find?"

Millie held back a smile. "Of course Stewart."

Stewart's silent permission emboldened Millie. She flew through chores with Sloane, ignoring the older girl's general irritability as they mucked stalls. She even bit her tongue when Sloane complained about the fallen tree "Can you even believe the state of this place—a tree fell on a clear night? It really should have been cut down if it was *that* rotten."

When Sloane took off in her car with the parting excuse that she was going to do inventory of the supply room, Millie saw her opportunity. She stepped out to take a cursory glance at the expectant mares, looking around to ensure she was alone on top of the hill.

Inside the tack room, she knew she had to be methodical in her search, going one section at a time, placing everything exactly where it came from, lest anyone arrive. If she was found, she decided to claim she had seen a roach go in whatever drawer or cabinet she had disassembled. *I suppose the coffee cabinet is as good a place as any to start.*

Millie wasn't sure what she was looking for, but didn't find it in the assorted variety of instant coffee and creamers, nor the eclectic collection of wires, broken hose nozzles, and single gloves. She huffed a sigh of frustration, running out to check the mares again. All that she was discovering was this farm had a serious problem with throwing away junk!

The medication and record books revealed no secrets, Millie's eyes crossing at all the various drug names—banamine, pentoxifylline, ciprofloxacin, and minocycline, how did anyone keep it all straight? Having peeked behind every bandage and snooped through every equine medical discharge letter, she stepped back with her hands on her hips.

She walked around the small room, dragging her gaze over every surface for whatever she was missing. She squinted her eyes at the crack between the fridge and the wall, sliding her hand in the narrow gap to feel around. A grin broke across her face as she grasped onto a square metal box wedged in.

After freeing the old tin box, she examined the small lock. Glancing out the door to make sure she was still alone, she pulled a hairpin out of her bun to manipulate the lock. It turned over easily, and Millie eagerly flipped it open to examine the contents. A small notebook sat on top.

DAYS SINCE LAST HAUNTING: 0

Came into work this morning and found the feed room ransacked. Stacks of feed pushed over, oil all over the place. I would have thought it was a raccoon or something, but the door was closed. Night watch had no clue what I was talking about.

DAYS SINCE LAST HAUNTING: 1

Last night on my 4—7 shift, I thought I was losing my mind. There were glowing white footprints leading away from the barn! It freaked me out so much that I locked myself in the tack room until Connie got here. When I tried to show her, they were gone.

DAYS SINCE LAST HAUNTING: 0

I've really got to stop taking these evening shifts. Eduardo had just left for the day when I started hearing maniacal laughter. Quiet, but definitely within the barn. I looked around but couldn't find anyone. The sound kept moving from one end of the barn to the other. It stopped around 5:30. Waiting for night watch to show up so I can go home and hopefully forget about this.

Millie frowned at the contents—most seemed to be dated within the last month, but a small handful were written over a year ago. In the bottom of the box was a folded piece of paper.

To: Sloane Oliver

From: Castledge Stud Farm, Australian division

Sloane, we wanted to personally thank you for your interest in our Broodmare Manager position at our flagship farm in New South Wales, Australia. We enjoyed speaking with you and learning about your impressive qualifications. Unfortunately, at this time our team did not select you for further consideration. We wish you the best of luck in your future endeavors and will be keeping your resume on file for any future openings we may have.

Regards,

Emma Peet

Human Resources Director

Castledge Stud Farm, Australian division

Millie jumped in surprise, hearing voices outside the barn. She quickly placed the notebook and paper back in the box, praying that she had wedged it back in the correct spot before turning out the lights and stepping outside. She looked around in confusion at the empty parking spots, the gentle rustle of wind in the bushes the only sound.

Chapter 15

"Is it okay if I borrow one of the farm trucks? I need to go to Oaklyn library after work to do some research on the farm."

"That's fine," Stewart replied, sounding distant. "Leave the night watch truck for 4—7, but you can take the maintenance truck."

"Okay," Millie agreed. "And if you can keep a secret, I have some intel for you."

"Really? About who?"

"I went through Sloane's things... Which is obviously a terrible thing to do. I feel kind of gross about it," she confided.

Stewart waved his hand flippantly. "All's fair in love and war, and all that. Morals are secondary when it comes to emergencies. I think this constitutes an emergency." He cleared his throat. "Anyways, what did you find out?"

"There were two pieces of evidence that I feel clear her of suspicion. First, a notebook detailing her own experiences with the 'hauntings', some entries dating back to over a year ago. And then, a job rejection letter from a stud farm in Australia!"

"Australia?!" He wrinkled his nose in confusion. "Has she ever mentioned any interest in going abroad to you?"

Millie shrugged. "We're not close, I doubt she would tell me. In any case, we need to keep this between us."

Stewart looked skeptical. "Are you sure that clears her? If she wants to leave, maybe she wants to take down the farm with her."

Millie shook her head. "I don't think so. The notebook is enough to convince me—someone has been messing with her as well. This week, she freaked out on me because she thought I had been messing with this year's foaling cards. Somehow the deceased mare cards got mixed up in this year's folder."

"Well, hopefully she doesn't get a new job before foaling season is over." He drummed his fingers on his steering wheel, deep in contemplation. "What are you looking for at the library?"

"I'm actually not sure," she admitted. "Pictures, news clippings, anything that might give me some insight into the farm's history."

"Better you than me. In high school, I was perpetually on the brink of flunking out of history class."

Millie changed the subject. "Has Chloe mentioned anything to you lately?"

"About what?" Stewart asked in confusion.

"Me," she offered sheepishly. "She confronted me a few days ago. Said I was ruining the farm with all my ghost talk. I was afraid to ask Jessica because I know they're friends."

Stewart snickered. "I haven't heard anything. I wouldn't let it bother you though. Chloe is always bent out of shape about something. She'll forget she's mad by tomorrow."

Millie grimaced as she spun the wheel to turn into the entrance of Oaklyn Racecourse. Though it dutifully plugged along for the fifteen minute drive, the maintenance truck left lots to be desired. The air conditioning didn't work, which would have been fine if three of the four windows hadn't been stuck closed, and the steering wheel had a looseness about it that always left you wondering if the white truck was ever actually going to turn.

She crossed over a stone bridge, looking around for signs indicating where the library was. The grounds of Oaklyn were green and immaculately landscaped. Old oaks towered over younger saplings, while dark green gate posts embossed with golden wreathed KR divided each side of the road.

Millie had been told so much about Oaklyn, she somehow expected it to be more bustling while it was in the midst of its Spring race meet. On a late weekday afternoon though, the grounds seemed all but abandoned.

The library was small and cozy, Millie imagined it would be the perfect place to spend time on a snowy winter day. Inside, she admired the dark walnut cabinets lining the walls and large, arched windows providing a golden light to the space. "Hi there," a petite woman called from the front desk. "Do you need help with anything?"

"I'm hoping you might be able to send me in the right direction," Millie began. "I was told you guys have lots of historic racing forms and sales records, but I was wondering if you keep any records of old farms in Fayette county?"

The woman frowned. "We definitely have historic photographs and news articles, but I'm afraid many of them aren't sorted, if you're looking for a particular farm."

Millie's heart sank. "I am, actually. I'm an intern at Willowmere Farm, off of Old Mill Road? Some of the barns are pretty old and I was interested in learning more about its history."

The woman brightened, smiling broadly. "Willowmere! That was a very prominent farm back in the seventies and early eighties, you should be able to find some information in our archives. I actually came across a few photos from there last week. It's in a big photo album though," she warned.

"That's okay, I don't mind doing a bit of digging," Millie enthused. "Would it be possible to look through the album?"

"Of course, we only ask that you handle it carefully. If you're interested in the Thoroughbred industry in that time period, you may enjoy our exhibit on the Oaklyn Yearling sale," she offered, gesturing to the next room over.

"Once I've worked through the photos, I'll be sure to take a look," Millie promised as the librarian led her into a small maze of bookshelves. The corner of the library was dark and still, the hard backed volumes filling the space with the rich scent of old pages. The librarian crouched down, squinting and scanning her finger over each spine."

"Here we are," she mumbled as she grasped a thick leather bound book. "We'll bring this over to the viewing area, it will be much more comfortable for you than sitting on the floor." She smiled, brushing a hand over the galloping horse embossed on the cover.

With the photo book placed on a long wooden table, the librarian turned to Millie. "Just let me know if you need any help, I'll be over at the front desk."

"Thank you so much," Millie smiled before grabbing a chair and diving into the old book. Black and white snapshots were pasted against a creamy backdrop, the captions dating most of the photos to the seventies. There were photos of horses, shed rows, a group of grooms clinging to one another laughing.

She flipped through as quickly as she could, though it was

easy to get lost in each photo. Each picture provided a window into one moment in time, and she found herself wondering where all these people were now. With a sobering thought, she realized that the barn cats, horses, friendly stable dogs, and even many of the people pictured, were gone now.

Millie's eyes were blurring with strain when she glanced at the large grandfather clock at the end of the table. Over an hour had passed and she wasn't even halfway through the book. *If I don't hurry, the library will close before I even finish this book.* She flipped the pages faster, reading the captions first in trying to not get sucked into the story that each photo told.

She flipped past two photos, then paused and went back to the first. It was a group of men, standing together laughing in the tunnel of Oaklyn's grandstand. The man in the middle stood tallest, seemingly caught mid sentence. Grasping his hand was a small boy, standing in front of his knees with a solemn expression. Something in the man's expression made Millie feel as though she knew him.

Oaklyn October Meet, opening day 1968
Jim Hattington (left), John McConnell (center), Timothy Charlotte (Right)

John McConnell! Millie recalled he was Riley's uncle, the man who was responsible for Willowmere being sold after his death. She must have seen his picture somewhere around the farm, she reasoned, that must be why he looked so familiar.

The next picture she flipped to was a familiar scene to her—looking up towards the Foaling Barn at Willowmere, taken from the large field that dips below it. Even in the black and white photo, you could see the hazy morning mist hanging over the bluegrass, murky sky giving it no chance to burn off. Though the trees were smaller, and it looked like the trim on the barn was a different color, it was instantly recognizable to Millie.

Morning of Willowmere end of season party, June 1966

Millie continued through the book but didn't find much else of note, aside from recognizing a few famous horses that appeared in the pedigrees of the mares she cared for now. With a sigh, she stood and stretched, glancing up the clock again. Thirty minutes to closing, she had just enough time to walk through the sales exhibit the librarian had told her about. Though the shadows had appeared, and then grown in the time Millie was there, the exhibit hall still had an airy brightness about it. Dark bronze statues of famous horses stood on the marble floor, their flared nostrils and popping veins lending them an eerie realism.

A glass display box held a wooden auction gavel, a tired looking sticker with 001 printed on it, and a pair of black leather gloves.

Mementos from the first Oaklyn September sale. Auction gavel, Hip sticker from 'Risky Business' (first horse ever sold), leather gloves worn by auction handler Barry Park.

She wandered around the room, reading the large poster boards explaining the auction process and history. At the top of the room, sat the largest display.

FIRST MILLION DOLLAR YEARLING

In 1976, Oaklyn hit an unprecedented milestone. A strong chestnut colt with four white stockings lit up the sales ring. The colt, eventually named Million Dreams, garnered international interest for his exceptional pedigree and outstanding physical appearance.

Sired by Secretariat, and out of the Hail to Reason

daughter Empress of Asia, he was bred and consigned by Willowmere Farm. Owner and manager John McConnell described the colt as "Lightning in a bottle. He has everything going for him—he comes from the right family, he walks great, and he has a really intelligent personality about him. My whole family feels very blessed to be a part of his career."

Purchased in partnership by Jackson Mitchell and First Run Thoroughbreds for $1,300,000, Million Dreams won one race in four starts, earning $11,286. With little success as a racehorse, he was gelded and found new purpose as a fox hunting mount for Mr. Mitchell's oldest daughter, Susannah.

Several photos of Million Dreams surrounded the display—in the sales ring, stretched out in a gallop crossing the finish line, and clearing a stone wall with a smiling girl astride. Millie leaned in to squint at the last photo, just a small black and white picture in a plain frame. The tall man—John McConnell—stood at Million Dreams' head, beaming at him with a hand resting on the colt's glossy neck. On his other side, a proud looking woman with sharp features and broad shoulders cracked a smile, looking over at John.

John McConnell and Anita Branson greet Million Dreams after being sold

Who was Anita Branson? Millie quickly added up the years in her head—she appeared to be in her early thirties in the photograph, so Anita would be in her late seventies or eighties by now, if she was still alive. The library clock chimed in warning, closing time had arrived. Millie sighed, glancing back at the small photo. It was time to go, but she already knew her next research project.

Millie sat behind the library in the idling truck. The sunset glowed pink and yellow, as if in celebration of another day completed. *Alan Westam bloodstock agent*, she pecked into the search engine in her phone, equal parts delighted and nauseous when she saw his phone number appear. Though she wanted to talk to him, a small part of her had been hoping that she would have to send an email, or talk to Jessica to get his information, so she would have more time to prepare. "Here goes nothing," she mumbled under her breath, pressing the call button.

"Hello?" a male voice answered.

"Hi, Alan? This is Millie Wright. We met a few days ago at Breezy Knoll, with Jessica?"

There was a pause on the line, Alan seeming confused. "Oh yes, hi Millie. What can I do for you?"

"I'm hoping you'll have some information for me. Last week when we went to Riley McConnell's place, it seemed like you knew the history surrounding his family?"

"That might be a bit of an overstatement. I've known Riley for many years, but we've never been close. Most of what I know about the farm is public knowledge."

"Just humor me please," she replied with a laugh. "You've got to know more than I do."

"Fair enough. What is it you're hoping to find out?"

"I was at the Oaklyn library just now. I looked through a photo book and walked through their exhibit on the September Yearling Sale. I found some pictures of John McConnell. Did you ever meet him?"

"I'm afraid I never got to. I've heard lots—really fun guy apparently. Threw lavish parties for the clients, that kind of thing. The main thing I've heard about him is that he was a real horseman down to his core. He really made a go of that farm—say what you like about having inherited it, but he took everything his family had and made it twice as good. They produced some outstanding horses at Willowmere during that era."

"So he had a good reputation, you'd say?"

"As far as I know. Never speak ill of the dead and all, perhaps he had a few skeletons in his closet like anyone else. I've only heard good things."

"Do you have any idea who Anita Branson is?"

"Anita Branson!" he bellowed with a burst of laughter. "I haven't heard that name in years. Is she still alive?"

"I have no idea," Millie admitted. "I came across a picture of her with John. I was hoping you would have some insight, or maybe a way to contact her."

Alan let out a sigh. "John and her were very close, they dated for a long time. She was a bloodstock agent, one of the first female agents to go solo. I think she got out of the horse industry after John passed."

"Did you know her well?" Millie pressed.

"I followed her at the sales a few times when I was starting out. She was kind to me, helped give me a leg up in the business. She was pretty sharp, nothing got by her. I'm afraid I haven't stayed in contact."

"Would you have any idea how to get a hold of her? Assuming she is still alive, of course." Millie bit back a remark about contacting her postmortem—she didn't know Alan well and figured you had to be familiar with the oddities of Willowmere for the joke to land.

"I don't, but I can put in a few calls to old friends if it would help you. Why are you interested in her again?" He inquired.

"Um... I'm doing some research on the history of Willowmere, and she was in a picture with the first ever million dollar yearling. I'm just curious mostly." Millie bit her lip, hoping her half truth would suffice.

"I don't believe she was ever involved in the day to day operations at the farm." he began skeptically.

"That's fine, I'll take whatever I can get."

"Okay Millie. I can do that. Not enough young people are interested in those who came before them, so good on you I suppose."

"I can't thank you eno—"

Alan cut her off. "I will warn you, Millie. At best, she will be elderly, and possibly unable to talk to you. Your homework is to search obituary records in the meantime. This may be a giant waste of time,"

"I know," Millie sang. "Let me know what you find out! And thank you again!"

Twilight had descended on the farm when Millie arrived back from the library. She left the truck at the maintenance building, walking at a brisk pace on the farm road towards her cottage. She glanced up at the ridge behind the Retirement Barn, noticing the darkened windows of Stewart's farmhouse.

Millie shivered, delighting in the cool air wrapping around her. The air smelled of honeysuckle and bluegrass, the stars growing brighter as the sky transitioned from deep purple to navy velvet. She closed her eyes for a moment, losing herself in the beauty of the moment. *What a perfect place...*

Her eyes flew open, hair on the back of her neck standing. Behind the hoots of an owl and the occasional drumming of hoof beats, was another sound. Millie stood, ears straining as she looked around through the darkness. A shovel struck soil time after time, disrupting the still of the evening.

Treading softly, she moved towards the sound, hoping the darkness would conceal her. Stepping behind a noble oak, she glanced around its thick trunk. A man in a navy shirt grunted with effort, swinging the shovel into the ground. He stopped for a moment, turning to the side to wipe his face.

Millie stepped out from behind the tree. "Whatcha doin', Stewart?" she asked, keeping her tone casual.

Stewart jumped in surprise, spinning around to face her. "Millie—what are you doing here?"

"Just walking home. Planting some tulips?"

Stewart huffed in frustration. "I swear, this isn't what it looks like."

Millie crossed her arms. "What does it look like?"

"Like, well, I don't know, Millie!" he exclaimed, throwing the shovel to the ground.

"Okay. So why don't you tell me what you were *actually* doing then? Unless you would rather tell the Jennings' instead?"

"No, no, no," he muttered, running a hand down his face. "I—I was looking for arrowheads."

Millie was skeptical. "You were looking for arrowheads? Why?"

"I collect them," he replied with an air of indignation. "Hobbies are important."

"I agree. Quick question though, why were you *digging* for them? I was under the impression that it was only legal to surface hunt for them."

Stewart grimaced. "Please don't tell anyone Millie. I swear I meant no harm."

Millie gave him a long, hard look. "I won't tell the Jennings' about it. You will. Because I hate to break it to you, but they're probably going to notice that half their lawn is completely dug up."

Stewart blinked, glancing down around himself. "Oh. Right. I'll fix it Millie. Don't worry."

"I'm sure." Millie walked down the drive, shaking her head. She had no idea what she had just stumbled upon, but it didn't sit well with her. She didn't think Stewart was behind the problems at the farm, but what other explanation was there for him being knee deep in a dirt pile after dark? She glanced back to make sure no one was following her before pulling out her phone to call Becca. "You're never going to believe what I just stumbled upon."

Chapter 16

Millie was grateful that mucking stalls was a relatively mindless task, because her mind couldn't have been further away. She kept replaying the previous night's events, wondering if she should have done something different, or pressed Stewart harder. She hadn't seen him today, perhaps he was avoiding her.

The night before when she got back to the house, she feigned exhaustion so she could go straight to bed. She didn't feel like telling Jessica about what she had seen, and figured it would be bad news if Stewart heard she was gossiping about him. With each pitchfork full of wet straw and manure, she came closer to calling Mr. Jennings to tell him what she had found out. Could Stewart even be trusted to run the farm? What was he actually doing?

Sloane was off today, so Millie was on her own to finish up the barn. Between Conquered having foaled a grey colt at 2 AM, and chores taking twice as long as usual, it felt like the morning would never end. She set down her fork and walked outside to check the mares, counting all the happy, swishing tails.

Her phone buzzed in her back pocket. "Hello?"

"Millie, it's Alan Westam. I found Anita."

Millie gasped in delight. "You did? How? Where is she?"

"I only had to make a few phone calls, she wasn't difficult to track down. Most importantly, she is alive and well. I spoke to her very briefly, but she doesn't like phones. She lives in an assisted living community in Callietown."

"Do you think she would be open to speaking with me?" Millie asked hopefully.

"I mentioned it and she agreed to speak with you, but only if I promised to visit her next week. I'll text you the phone number after we hang up."

"Oh Alan," she cringed. "I'm sorry. I didn't realize you would get roped into going to visit her, I know you're very busy."

Alan laughed. "Oh, I don't mind. I'm actually looking forward to seeing her. It's hard to tell over the phone, but she still sounded sharp as a tack. In any case, I know exactly how you can repay me for this."

Millie winced. Between her job and investigation, she had practically no free time, but knew she couldn't turn Alan down after he had tracked down Anita just for her. She swallowed, smoothing her voice out. "Of course, whatever you need."

"You see, Riley McConnell started bothering me again about these yearlings he has for sale. He wants me to come look at one filly in particular, but he's requesting I bring my photographer with me. Honestly, I don't think she's going to be worth the price of printer paper, so I don't want to pay for my guy to drive out to Lyon with me."

Millie wasn't sure where he was going with his request. "Okay? Where do I come in?"

"Well," he began. "I thought you did such a great job with pictures last time, we could just set you up again with one of

137

my old DSLR cameras, maybe put a big lens on to look fancy." Millie snorted. "Sure Alan, but a photographer I am not."

"Don't worry about it," he advised. "I'll call Jessica and ask her to bring you to Lyon at 4:30. Does that work?"

"Of course."

Millie frowned at the darkening sky as she led the last mare into the barn for the night. A gust of wind blew, and Conquered danced sideways, her eyes wide as she looked around for her newborn colt. "Easy," Millie cooed to the lanky mare, "He's right behind you, just keep walking now."

After the pair was safely locked in their stall, Millie felt a deep satisfaction. All fourteen mares were put away for the evening, with deep bedding, piles of green alfalfa hay, and crystalline water buckets. Rain was just now beginning to drum on the roof, and she still had an hour until work was over.

She was preparing the supplements and medicine for the mares when Stewart pulled his truck into the barn. Millie's spine tightened involuntarily. "Hey Stewart." Her voice sounded uneven when she spoke, and she internally chastised herself. *Act normal.*

"Millie, I was just coming up here to help you get everything in before the storms hit. Looks like you've got it under control though."

She smiled tightly. "They're all set for the night, I'm finishing up medications and the log books. Drama Queen is the only one that I think is really close, she seemed uneasy in the field this afternoon."

There was an awkward pause, the two facing each other but not speaking. Stewart cleared his throat. "I also wanted to apologize for last night. I realize I put you in an awkward position."

Millie gave a curt nod. "Thank you. Now are you going to tell me what you were really up to?"

He shook his head in remorse. "I promise you, I will tell the Jennings' when they get back."

"That didn't answer my question."

"Fine. So maybe I got a little caught up in the whole mystery of the farm."

Millie looked at him quizzically. "Don't tell me you were looking for pirate gold or something."

Stewart shook his head sheepishly. "There are these numbers written in weird places in my house. Like, inside cabinets and closets, they seemed to make up coordinates when you put them all together. I don't know what I thought I was looking for. I just rearranged things until they made sense, found the spot, and started digging."

Millie thought this sounded as flimsy as his arrowhead excuse. "What made you start digging? Why didn't you, say, look up and chart the constellations in the sky? Or look for a clue in the trees?"

To his credit, Stewart looked embarrassed. "I don't know. Isn't 'X marks the spot' the most classic treasure hunting trope of all time?"

Millie smiled ruefully. "Who said anything about treasure?"

Stewart shrugged. "I mean, one of the variations of the story about the Lockhurst Lady is that she comes back to protect her jewels and valuables. Who knows if there's any truth to it, obviously."

Millie groaned. "You've got to be kidding me. First of all, that sounds absolutely ridiculous. Secondly, historic jewels might just give someone enough of a reason to try and drive people off the farm—you never thought to mention it?"

Stewart cringed. "I see how bad this looks."

"Just please be truthful with me from here on out," she sighed.

Stewart nodded, staring straight ahead for a moment. "I forgot to tell you earlier, Lena Fever and her filly are coming home tomorrow afternoon. In the morning, I'll need you to bed down a stall in quarantine for them."

"Of course," she agreed, trying to hide her smile.The pair would have a long road ahead, but discharge from the hospital was the first step on the staircase to recovery.

"Oh. You girls again?" Riley said, visibly disappointed as they walked into the barn.

Millie could feel Jessica tense next to her. She had been in a foul mood since picking up Millie from the Foaling Barn after work. Alan had called ahead to let her know what was going on, ruining her rainy afternoon plans of watching Gilmore Girls reruns from under a blanket. Millie had offered to take the dilapidated maintenance truck, but Jessica had refused. "No," she assured her. "If that truck spontaneously combusts while you're driving, I don't want it to be on my conscience. Anyways, Uncle Alan asked me himself. If I weasel my way out of it, I'll never hear the end of it."

Millie pushed her shoulders back and pasted a bright smile on her face. "Mr. McConnell! Lovely to see you again. Alan will be here in just a moment."

He gave a curt nod, then stalked back into the barn office. Millie frowned, what had gotten into everyone? She knew the sky was getting darker, but it wasn't raining here yet!

Alan's sedan pulled up next to Jessica's jeep, Millie smiling and waving while Jessica sulked over her phone.

"Hi girls!" he shouted in a chipper tone as he dug through the trunk of his car. "I'm just looking for your camera," he announced in a stage whisper. "I know it's back here somewhere."

"You don't know where the photographer's camera is?" she hissed. "What if the battery is dead?"

"It will be fine, I'm sure of it," he waved her off.

"He was annoyed that Jessica and I showed up," she warned.

"He'll have to get over it."

A ray of sunshine broke through the dark clouds, giving the farm a hazy look. Alan handed Millie a camera. "I honestly don't know how to work this very well, but the off and on buttons are up top there, and you can disengage the flash mode here." he clapped his hands together. "Who's ready to take some pictures?!"

Millie wracked her brain for everything she had learned during a photography workshop the previous summer. Alan went ahead inside to speak with Riley, leaving her to figure out the camera. It had a thirty-five percent charge, so Millie knew she had to move quickly during the shoot. She looked around at the scenery of the tired farm. She needed a spot with level ground and a neutral background for the photos.

She found a nice spot on the driveway with a classic Kentucky black fence background, away from the clutter of the farmyard. With the emerging sunshine, she positioned herself with her back facing the light. Turning on the camera, she set it to high resolution and chose landscape mode, figuring a horse would be too long for a good portrait style photo.

The two men led a gleaming bay filly with a white stripe out of the barn, one of the first horse's she had seen on her original visit. "I'm ready whenever you are," she called out.

Riley paused. "You're the photographer?" he asked, his tone short. "Why didn't you use your camera when you were here last time? An iPhone isn't flattering for anyone."

"It was at the repair shop," she covered up. "I take lots of pictures for Alan."

"She is very talented," Alan added brightly. "And Jessica has lots of experience helping to set horses up for conformation pictures. Why don't you go ahead and take your filly for a walk, so I can look at her?"

Jessica crept up next to Millie. "As Riley holds the horse, I'll be right there, readjusting her hooves so she looks perfectly balanced. We want all four legs to be visible, with the near side legs perpendicular to the ground, and the far side legs placed slightly under the body. Balance is the most important thing, the horse can't look like they're leaning forward or back."

Millie blinked at her. "I had no idea so much went into it," she muttered. "I thought you just took a picture whenever the horse stopped."

Jessica snickered quietly. "It's okay, that's why I told you. Riley will never know you haven't done this before."

The filly, Chocolate Candy, bounced and pranced next to Riley, flipping her head towards the sky. She looked like a bird ready to take flight, and Millie wondered dimly if portly Riley with his mild limp would be any match for her. Thankfully, she didn't have to find out. Chocolate Candy dropped her head and allowed her stride to flow forward. She was a nice filly, Millie thought, with long, clean lines, a powerful hip, and an attractive head.

"Okay, great," Alan called out. "You think she's ready for her picture? I figure we can set her up in front of the barn?"

Millie shook her head. "No, she'll be standing in the shadows there, I want her in the sunlight. Let's go in front of the pasture fence along the drive there."

Alan grinned, raising his hands in submission. "Whatever you say young lady, you're the expert here."

Riley grimaced but went where he was directed, carefully stepping the filly forward and back until she was in a proper open stance. "Jessica," Alan called out. "Bring that left front a hair forward, will you?"

Jessica walked up to the filly with care, speaking softly and resting a hand on her shoulder before running it down her leg. When Jessica squeezed, Chocolate Candy flicked her tail in irritation, taking two unbalanced steps back. Everyone groaned it unison, while Riley tried to pull her back up to the correct stance.

This continued on long enough for Millie to consider throwing the camera onto the hard packed gravel so it would break and she could go home. "Does this always take so long?" she asked Alan through gritted teeth.

Alan's eyes glittered with laughter. "Every single time, Millie. I think I can count on one hand how many times a yearling has come out and stood itself up correctly on the first shot. Which is why it's so important for the photographer to *always* be paying attention." He gestured knowingly at the filly, whose pinned back ears were the only thing ruining the otherwise perfect shot.

Out of nowhere, a massive vulture dove into the tall grass on the other side of the fence, crinkling in the foliage as it landed. Chocolate Candy's eyes looked like they were about to pop out of her head. Millie pressed the camera shutter an instant before the filly shot forward as if ejected from a cannon. Pressing the playback button on the camera, "I think I got it!"

she announced.

From there, it all seemed to happen in slow motion, the lead shank slipping through Riley's hand, sending him stumbling forward before face planting in the drive. The filly dove to the right, dodging Riley's fallen frame, fleeing the scene with her tail flagged. "Oh my gosh," Millie exclaimed, jogging over to him. "Are you okay? Can you wiggle your fingers and toes?"

"Ugh," Riley groaned, sitting up. "*I'm* perfectly fine. Why don't you and your assistant go track down that filly before she hurts herself? Especially because we would have been done by now if it weren't for your *incompetence*."

Millie flew back as if she had been slapped. She wanted to give him a piece of her mind, but bit her tongue in the interest of catching the filly, who had found an especially lush patch of grass to spend her time on.

Jessica and Millie approached to filly from opposite sides, locking eyes in a silent agreement of their plan. They stretched their arms out to make themselves appear wider, slowly herding the filly towards the fence line. Chocolate Candy snatched at the grass frantically, angling her head to watch the girls as she stuffed her mouth. As they approached closer, she trotted a few halfhearted steps to the fence before dropping her head back to the grass. "You stay there," Jessica muttered under her breath. "I'm going to try and get to her head."

Jessica crept forward, slouching her posture to appear less threatening. She extended out a hand to the quivering filly. "Easy girl, just stay still for a minute,"

Jessica grasped the lead shank hanging under the filly's chin, and patted her with her free hand. Millie let out a sigh of relief, glancing over at Alan and Riley standing a short distance away. Riley looked irritated, with his jaw tense and arms crossed, but

Millie thought he was a little hard to take seriously, still covered in stone dust.

"Nice job," Alan praised as Jessica led Chocolate Candy by.

"We're done with her, right?" she called out, pausing before she entered the stable.

"All done," Alan confirmed. *And not a moment too soon*, Millie thought to herself.

Riley looked to Millie expectantly. "When can I expect to see those pictures, young lady?"

Millie froze—she didn't even know how she was going to download the pictures from the camera, let alone edit the photos. "About a week," she replied smoothly. She hoped that would be plenty of time to figure out how to work with editing software!

"As soon as we have everything together, I'll start putting out feelers for clients who may want to purchase privately," Alan explained. "If you end up wanting to run her through the auction in September, we will want to get updated pictures late in the summer."

"Of course," Riley agreed. "But hopefully we won't have to."

"You're wanting a quick sale then?"

Riley smiled ruefully. "I know I need a new roof on this barn this summer, and I would like her to help pay for it."

Alan nodded. "Understood."

Jessica walked out of the barn and approached them. "I put her in the empty stall at the end of the shed row," she told Riley.

"Thank you," Riley glared.

"Well, anyhow, it was nice seeing you Riley. I'll be in touch," Alan reached his hand out towards Riley.

The girls muttered thank you's as they crept back to the car wordlessly. Alan paused by the back, glancing to make sure

Riley was gone. "I can take the camera and edit the pictures if you like, Millie,"

"Thank you," she sighed out with relief.

"No, thank *you*," he laughed under his breath. "If you hadn't agreed to do this, I would have had to pay someone."

Millie snickered. "It would have been fine, you just would have had to take that out of your commission."

Alan grimaced. "I have a feeling there won't be a commission. She's a nice enough filly, but not a standout."

Jessica snorted. "I hope she sells so she can get out of that barn."

Alan and Millie turned towards her in question. "That barn is disgusting. Manure packed in the stalls, the water smells foul."

Alan shook his head. "I had no idea."

"Is he having financial troubles?" Millie inquired.

Alan rubbed his jaw uncomfortably. "Not that I'm aware of. But," he continued, gesturing around them. "I can't imagine he's swimming in cash, judging by the state of this place."

Jessica sighed at them, apparently bored with the discussion. "Didn't you know? He just bounced a check to Mr. Freedey for a load of hay."

Alan looked taken aback. "What? Where did you hear that?"

"Last week at the feed mill," Jessica drawled. "Mr. Freedey came storming in to ask Jeannette if Riley's account was still in good standing. She said he hadn't ordered feed in months, figured he was getting it somewhere else."

"I had no idea," He glanced back at the barn worriedly. "I hope he hasn't got himself into too much trouble."

"Not to worry," Jessica smirked. "You're going to sell that filly for him and get him back on track, right?"

"Right," he echoed. "No pressure or anything."

Millie listened to their banter halfheartedly. She was itching to call Anita and find out what she knew. The sky was turning dark again, a green tinged cloud overhead giving the parking lot an ominous tinge. "I think we need to get going before we get flooded in."

Alan glanced upwards. "I think that's a good call, Millie. Thank you girls again. I'm sure we'll see each other soon."

Chapter 17

Millie sat on the front porch swing holding her cell phone to her ear, her bare feet hanging off the edge. The sound of water dripping off the eaves was the only clue a massive storm had rolled through Central Kentucky, the sunset bathing the rolling hills in a soft yellow light.

"So you survived photography duty?" Joe teased.

Millie let out a huff. "You have no idea. And just after I got the shot, the filly got loose! Riley seemed really angry."

"He'll get over it," he reassured her. "It would be impossible to hold a grudge against a photographer as charming as you."

"Shut up," Millie snickered before turning her tone serious. "Do you know if there's any good reason for someone to be digging holes along the drive near Field 14?"

"Um, this sounds like a loaded question."

"It is," Millie replied briskly.

"As far as I know, nothing is there. Can I ask why?"

Millie paused, considering her next words. "Can you keep a secret?"

The line was silent for a moment. "Of course."

"I found Stewart digging there last night, just after dusk. He wouldn't tell me what he was doing and he avoided me all day.

When I confronted him, he had some half baked excuse about 'looking for treasure'. It feels wrong, but I can't have this getting around the farm. If he caught wind of it, he would know it came from me."

Joe took a moment to gather his thoughts. "Maybe you should watch out around him, Millie."

"I'm careful around everyone, you know that," she retorted.

Millie pulled her phone away, frowning at the call waiting beep as Joe rambled on about some oil leak somewhere. "Joe," she cut him off. "Sorry, but I have to take this, I think it's Anita calling me back!"

"Who?" he asked. "I guess I'll talk to you tomorr—"

"Hello?" Millie answered.

"IS THIS MILLIE WRIGHT?" a too loud voice bellowed.

Millie winced. "This is she. May I ask who's calling?"

"THIS IS ANITA BRIGHTON RETURNING YOUR CALL, Millie. IS THIS A GOOD TIME?"

"Yes, yes, it's perfect. Is there any chance you could, erm, move the phone away from your mouth a little? I'm hearing... lots of static."

"LIKE THIS?"

"Perfect." Millie muttered, moving the phone away from her ear. "I was hoping to ask you some questions about John McConnell and his farm, if you'd be willing."

Anita drew a sharp breath in. "That was a long time ago sweetie,"

"Anything you can remember would be helpful," Millie urged. "Anything at all."

Anita let out a bark of laughter. "I remember lots. It's just figuring out where to start."

"Let's start with John," Millie encouraged. "What was he like?"

"John was a real charmer. He had a way of making everyone feel really special... I think that's why he was so good at sales. Always remembered whose horse had won a race three months earlier, who got married over the summer."

"You and him were involved?"

Anita paused. "We dated for almost ten years."

"Never wanted to get married?" Millie inquired.

Anita laughed. "I wouldn't say we didn't *want* to. But we were so busy back then. I secretly worried that he was going to wake up one day and realize he was sick of being with a bloodstock agent, not seeing me for two weeks at a time. We maintained separate residences but usually I ended up living at his farm."

"What can you tell me about the farm?"

"I wasn't involved in the day to day operations, but I spent lots of time there. The manager's house was so big and drafty. It was always creaking and groaning, I was so convinced there were spirits living in the attic. I was always begging John to let us move into the assistant's house because it was smaller. He never agreed though, I think because he liked having that extra space for Riley—that was his nephew."

"Did Riley spend much time with you guys?"

"Oh yeah, he was with us through most of the summer usually and sometimes a good chunk of the school year. His dad was a bit of a deadbeat as I recall, and I don't think his mom was real interested in being a mom, ya know? He loved the farm, always upset when he had to leave. Not having kids of our own, John and I always liked to spoil him a bit, let him tag along with us everywhere like a little adult. Once he got a bit older, John let him work on the farm, he liked that a lot."

"You and Riley were close then?" Millie asked, trying to piece together the puzzle in her mind.

Anita laughed. "Hardly! Riley resented me, if anything. I'm sure in his mind, I was the horrible woman standing between him and his wildest dreams. He had John wrapped around his little finger, and I was always the one playing bad cop."

"Really?!" Millie replied in shock. "How so?"

"There was always *something*, especially as a teenager. Riley would get himself into trouble over stupid little things—dinging someone's car and then driving off, falling asleep at work after staying out too late—and John was always there to catch him if he fell. I remember John and I would get into big fights over it, like we were his parents or something!

"When Riley flunked out of college, John said to come to Willowmere and be his assistant manager. I fought tooth and nail, saying it was a horrible idea. He had no horsemanship experience aside from what he had learned working summers in the yearling barns! He wouldn't have known how to differentiate between a colic and a mare about to foal if his life depended on it! In the end, Riley got his way of course and moved into the little assistants house. I heard plenty of mutters around town, but I guess he did a decent enough job because the place never burnt down or anything."

"How long did he stay at Willowmere then?"

"Until John passed away, about three years."

Millie took a deep breath. "Anita... if you don't mind me asking. How did John pass away?"

"It's fine honey, it was a lifetime ago." She reassured Millie with a sigh. "He had a brain aneurysm in his sleep. Went to bed early the night before, he had gotten into some argument with Riley. Said he had a headache, and then never woke up. I was in England at the Pattersail auction when I got the call."

"That's horrible... I'm so sorry, Anita."

"It's all right, doll. I think for the most part, he led a happy life. I spoke to him the night before he passed and he seemed content. He loved the land and the horses, and got to live a life surrounded by them. Isn't that the best someone could ever hope for?"

Millie sat for a moment, trying to let her words seep in. "Yes, I suppose it is." She cleared her throat. "Can you tell me anything about the aftermath of that? Did you keep in touch with Riley?"

Anita let out a sad laugh. "Absolutely not. There was no love lost between the two of us. Knowing him, he probably thought I deliberately had John cut him out of the will. Which, by the way, is absolutely not the case. We weren't married, so I wasn't necessarily expecting anything, but I was surprised as anyone by how things turned out."

Now we're getting somewhere, Millie thought to herself. "You got *nothing*?" She grilled Anita. "Where did everything go then? I heard the farm was auctioned off, but nothing about his other assets."

"All of it to charity for retired racehorses and disabled jockeys. He always worried so much about all the horses coming off his farm, what would happen if they couldn't run. I suppose the writing was on the wall, but I was astounded. I assumed that Riley would get everything since John had no children and wasn't close with his brother."

"He never mentioned *anything* about his will?"

"Nothing. It remains one of the great mysteries of my life. I wish he would have trusted me enough to tell me, just so I wasn't surprised. For the record, I think it was as good of a use for the money as any. I didn't need it and Riley wasn't prepared for his own farm."

"How did Riley handle that?"

"He was upset. He had talked about contesting the will, claiming the one on file with John's attorney was old. I don't think it ever went anywhere. Remember, Riley was little more than a kid when this all happened."

"Do you think that John may have left additional money or valuables somewhere that wasn't mentioned in the will?"

Anita sounded taken aback. "Why, the thought has never crossed my mind. Why do you ask?"

Millie chewed her bottom lip in deliberation. "I've heard lots of rumors around this farm, we'll just put it that way."

"Well," Anita mused. "I doubt it, but it's not the craziest thing I've ever heard. Maybe down in those disgusting tunnels he would never let Riley go in."

Millie's heart skipped. "Tunnels? You know about that?"

"Of course I did. John thought they were the coolest thing. The first time he took me into one, I told him to never, ever bring me again… It was dark, and musty, and I remember I kept walking through cobwebs. Wait a second… how do *you* know about the tunnels, young lady?"

"It was a complete accident!" Millie sputtered. "I followed a calico cat out to a tree, next thing I know I'm climbing a ladder down into one."

"I hope you encountered fewer creepy crawlies than I did! Funny about the calico though. There used to be dozens around that farm. Pretty things, but an over abundance of them. Maybe the one you met is a descendant."

"I suppose it's possible," Millie mused. "Do you know what the purpose of the tunnel is?"

"I'm not exactly sure, but John's grandfather, who built the place? He was a paranoid character. I believe they were dug around the time of World War II. No idea if they were meant as a shelter or a hiding spot, but they never got much use either way. Riley was always begging to go into them, but John was rightfully afraid they were going to collapse on him."

"Was there more than one tunnel?"

"I'll only tell you if you promise not to go looking for it!" Anita warned. "Those things were old and decrepit when I lived there, and that was a long time ago girl!"

"Of course, of course," Millie promised. She tried to not think too hard about the moral code of lying for the greater good.

"There were at least two I believe, maybe more. Like I said, he took me to one that connected to the crawlspace of the house, and believe me when I say I was unamused. 'Never again, John!' were my exact words."

"Did you ever experience anything spooky, or weird at the farm?"

"Aside from the graveyard behind the house? It was a spooky place and came with a long list of legends, I'll give you that. But I don't think anything too weird ever happened. Normal stuff, like shoes going missing and doors blowing open. Why?"

"Let's just say I think someone is trying to blame a ghost for something much more... *earthly* that's going on here."

"Come on, you've grilled me. Now, you have to tell me what's happening there to make you so interested in an old biddy like me."

"Well, for starters," Millie began, "Our night watchman quit on the spot, claiming that there was a ghost controlling the lights and radio. Then I got switched to night watch duty, where I saw a glowing white figure walking across a field. *Then,* something carved 'leave this farm now' into the front doors of the yearling barn. Oh, and a large ditch was dug inside a filly pasture, deliberately covered with netting and leaves to disguise it."

All humor had left Anita's voice. "Oh my gosh," she muttered. "That sounds serious."

"It is," Millie confided. "I've been given instructions to keep all of it under wraps, but people talk. It's getting around town."

"The Jennings' still own and run it, right?" Anita pondered. "They came along after my time, so I don't know them. I've heard good things though. It's a little sad to think the farm was sold outside of the family, but it sounds like they've done a nice job."

"Yes, they still own it. I'll be honest, I still haven't met them—Mr. Jennings has been stuck in the hospital and his wife hasn't left his side."

"The hospital? Whatever for? I hope he's okay." Anita asked worriedly.

"I wasn't there for it, but some colts got loose in the middle of the night. Mr. Jennings was called out, and ended up getting trampled while trying to catch them. He's banged up pretty badly, but is supposed to come home soon."

"How did the colts get loose?"

Millie hesitated. "Like I said, I wasn't there. I heard that the gate was left open, but I may have gotten some details wrong. I understand it was quite the scene, especially once an ambulance was called."

"Millie," Anita began firmly. "I don't know you, but as someone who has been around the block a few times, I want to give you some advice. I think you need to get yourself out of this situation."

"I don't think that's necess—"

Anita cut her off. "Millie. You've already told me at least one person has been seriously injured. Strange things are happening everywhere. I understand you want to do a good job and learn everything, but you need to draw a line somewhere. The horse business can be cutthroat, that's a big reason why I left. Understand?"

Millie gulped. "Of course. Thank you for your time—it was very informative."

After exchanging goodbyes, she ended the call and looked out over the darkening retiree pasture. Two old mares hobbled across the hill to the automatic waterer. Millie watched, hypnotized by their steady footfalls, and shook her head. Maybe the ghost of Willowmere farm wasn't her problem after all.

Chapter 18

"What's wrong with you?" Joe called as she shuffled up to the maintenance building.

"Nothing," Millie mumbled, her eyes downcast.

"I'm going to avoid the temptation to make a joke here, and seriously ask you if you're okay?"

Millie stared at him, unblinking, until she felt hot tears threatening to spill. *Knock it off,* she chided herself. *Hold it together, Wright.* She wasn't sure why she sometimes felt so emotional around him, but she never wanted him to find out.

"Millie, you're making me worried now."

"Fine!" she snapped at Joe. "Is there somewhere we can talk?"

He raised an eyebrow, looking around at the abandoned shop. He thought better of asking why they had to move, and instead lead her to the office, gently shutting the door behind her. "Have I done something?" he asked, perplexed.

"No," she shook her head. "I think I need to leave the farm."

Joe looked mildly surprised. "Okay. Talk me through why."

Millie's eyes flickered everywhere but his face. When she spoke, her voice was small, birdlike. "I talked to Anita Brighton last night, she used to live here when John McConnell owned it. I had to tell her some of the things that have been happening.

She said I was crazy for staying here. Joe, I don't know, when I had to lay it all out for her, an uninvolved stranger, I saw everything clearly. It's not safe for me to be poking around. I should go back to Vermont for the summer, work in my parents' gift shop or something."

Joe's eyebrows drew together, concerned. "Hey now," he reassured her, "You don't have to decide this right now. Take a day, think it over."

"I have thought it over," she wailed. "What kind of person sticks around after seeing a literal ghost?!" Joe fought a grin, and suddenly Millie was laughing. "It's ridiculous, isn't it?"

Joe took a deep breath. "I don't think there are any wrong decisions here. I bet you don't even have to leave Kentucky if you don't want to. You heard Chuy when we visited, all the farms need help these days. Or, you could give it a few more days here. If you do want to go home, I understand."

Millie nodded, deep in thought. "I guess I hadn't thought of finding another internship out here."

"If you need a reference, you know I'll vouch for you," he offered.

She hesitated. "If I do go home, can we stay in touch?"

Joe smiled, reaching his hand out to grasp hers. "Of course."

Walking away, Millie reminded herself to keep her breath slow and even. She wasn't ready to talk to anyone else about her doubts. She knew her mother would demand her safe return to Vermont, and Stewart would insist she stay. But, she reasoned with herself, wouldn't it be more appropriate to give her notice to the Jennings', since they're who hired her, and still technically her boss?

Millie braced her jaw. She would wait for the Jennings' to get back to the farm in just a day or two, then she would inform them of her decision. That would give her time to ponder her next move, whether she remained in the bluegrass or headed back towards the green mountains.

She glanced at her watch, quickening her pace. Lunch was almost over, and she still had to get past the Yearling Barn and climb up the hill towards the Foaling Barn. Sloane was usually late getting back from lunch, but became irritated when others did the same. Thinking about the stack of dirty water buckets and feed tubs calling her name did nothing to improve her enthusiasm.

Stewart's navy truck pulled up beside her, Millie internally groaning as he rolled down his window. "Need a ride?"

"Sure," she agreed, begrudgingly walking around to the passenger door of the truck and hopping in.

They sat in a tense silence before Stewart spoke, his eyes staring straight ahead. "I'm going to need you to cover the 4—7 shift tonight."

Millie sat for a moment. She felt like a wrung out dishrag, tired of dealing with other people's problems. Her voice was steady when she replied. "No."

Stewart pursed his lips, still staring ahead intently as they began to climb the hill. "You are an intern who lives on the farm without your own vehicle. Chloe just quit out of nowhere, so I am telling you to do it."

"Stewart," Millie began, her tone heated. "How is it *my* fault that Chloe just quit? I have been filling in left and right since I started here. Why is it that no one else ever has to? I had plans for this evening and never would have agreed to it before, never mind now that it's a few hours away."

The truck slammed to a stop, Stewart turning to her with a

crazed look. "Millie, I don't think you get it," he spit out. "It's all hands on deck right now. I need you to do this, end of story. Understand?"

Millie's eyebrows shot up, sitting quietly in the shock of Stewart's outburst. There was a strange buzzing in the air, Millie vaguely wondering if she somehow misinterpreted his aggression. "That's fine," she confirmed in a measured tone. "But I would suggest *never* speaking to me that way again."

She threw open the door and got out, Stewart apparently realizing his mistake. "Millie, Millie, I'm sorry, there's been so much going on—"

Millie ignored him, striding through the side door of the barn. When she heard the roar of his truck driving away, she felt a wave of relief. The altercation had left her oddly invigorated, like a heavy weight had been lifted from her shoulders. *I don't have to feel like a horrible person for quitting anymore,* she told herself with glee.

She was practically skipping by the time Sloane arrived late. "What's with you?" the older girl questioned.

"Not much, just really excited to get these buckets cleaned."

Sloane rolled her eyes with disdain. "I'll leave you to it. I need to run to the office. Don't forget to check the mares, and Wonderstruck's foal needs her medicine at 3 o'clock."

Millie nodded obediently, biting back retorts about being left alone to do all the afternoon chores. *These won't be my problems for long.*

Her arms and back ached as she scrubbed, and she wondered if the scent of ivory soap was going to become a permanent part of her. The menial task helped settle her mind, and she was lulled into a better mood. Standing back with her hands on her hips, she admired the thirty freshly scrubbed water buckets and feed tubs. She rinsed her hands off, sighing as she realized she would have to hang them back up.

Millie let herself fall into the familiar rhythm of hanging buckets, dragging around the perpetually leaking hose to fill water buckets, and mixing and dumping individually made buckets of sweet feed, in between quick walks outside to check the expectant mares. She hummed and swayed a bit as she mixed and dispensed medication for the afternoon, comfortable in the knowledge she was alone in the stable.

Feed and medication swung alongside her as she walked down to the paddocks. Sloane had texted her directions to feed the mares with foals outside so they could stay out overnight because of the mild weather. "Fewer stalls to clean tomorrow," she sang to the birds.

Millie set the bucket of feed outside the paddock gate and went in, hiding the syringe full of medication behind her back. "Hey guys!" she called out as the mare and foal looked on with suspicion from the opposite side of the paddock.

Freshly mowed grass whispered under her feet as she made her way towards the pair. Wonderstruck snorted with concern, but stood while Millie grabbed the chin piece of her halter to still her. The dark foal clamped her tail down and ducked underneath her mother.

Millie let out a huff of frustration, directing the mare towards the fence. The foal tottered along next to her happily as Millie positioned Wonderstruck so the filly was trapped between the mare and the fence. She glared at her with wide eyes, disbelieving that she was really trapped. Before she could dive under her dam again, Millie let go of the mare and got her arm around the foal.

The filly shot forward and squirmed every which way, but

Millie held firmly. At last she stopped, her tiny nostrils and chest heaving with exertion. "Was that so awful?" Millie cooed as she scratched her withers, the filly leaning into her touch. She felt a pang of sadness as she fussed over the foal—she wouldn't be able to see the wobbly newborns develop into strong sucklings once she left.

With the filly relaxed, Millie gently inserted her thumb into the corner of her mouth, opening it just wide enough to fit the syringe. In one quick motion, she inserted it and depressed the plunger before the filly had time to react. The filly was irritated with the turn of events, pinning her ears and striking out her front leg as medicine dripped from her soft muzzle. Millie giggled as she continued stroking her neck.

Suddenly, the filly bolted forward as if shot from a cannon. Millie held on for several strides, the mare galloping past them, until she had to let go. Once released, the filly stretched her neck out and threw out a violent kick, connecting with Millie's shin. Millie gasped in pain, stumbling forward before letting herself fall slowly.

"Darn you," she muttered between gritted teeth, clutching her shin. Experimentally, she wiggled her toes and moved her leg around. She figured she would have a heck of a bruise the next day, but didn't think she was seriously hurt. She stared at the sky for a long moment, closing her eyes towards the gentle breeze.

I need to get moving, she chided herself. There were still pregnant mares to bring inside, and she wanted to visit with Lena Fever and her foal in the Quarantine Barn. Gathering herself to stand, she felt the hair on the back of her neck prickle.

Freezing, she looked around, her heart jumping as she saw movement in the grass. Less than five feet away, a brown snake raised its head and made eye contact with Millie.

Millie and the snake stared at one another, both unmoving. Hands shaking, she studied the snake, trying her best to recall everything she had learned about reptiles from wildlife camp as a child. Her eyes flicked to its hourglass shaped patches and triangular shaped head—a textbook copperhead.

Millie was terrified the snake would think she was attacking if she moved, so she remained in the grass with her unsteady breathing. After a moment had passed, the snake dropped its head back to the ground and slithered away towards the fence. Millie scrambled to her feet, wincing at the pain radiating from her shin.

Wonderstruck and her foal stood by the gate, looking at Millie as if she had lost her mind. "Don't harass me about dinner," she warned. "This was all your fault, little one!"

Chapter 19

With two soft muzzles gently nudging her hands, Millie wished she could spend her entire 4—7 shift here. Sitting cross legged in the straw with Lena's sprawled out filly, she glanced at her watch and groaned. 5:08 p.m. *Only one hundred and twelve more minutes until I'm done,* Millie told herself wistfully.

She had a pounding headache, and her shin still ached from where Wonderstruck's foal had kicked her. The exciting buzz from her argument with Stewart had worn off, and now she just felt tired. Dinner, a shower, and a TV movie were all she wanted.

"I should leave you two alone so you can properly rest," she told the mare and foal. "I sure am glad you're both okay though,"

Lena offered a soft whicker as Millie rubbed the white star on her forehead. She crouched back down to the foal, frowning as her fingers caught on the filly's IV catheter sewn into her neck. "That will be gone soon enough," she assured the filly. "Once you're a little stronger, and all done with your medications and fluids, there's a field full of other foals that can't wait to meet you. I need you to be a good girl and focus on getting better though, okay?"

The filly, who was beginning to look like a perfect replica of her dam, blinked sleepily at Millie. Straw clung to her soft mane as she dropped her head to lay flat out in the stall. Laughing, Millie stood and let herself out of the stall. "I'll take that as a hint, girls."

Shutting off the lights, she glanced at the cameras on her phone but all the mares seemed quiet. Before she had left that afternoon, Sloane told her it would probably be several days until the next foal. *If I finish my rounds now, all that I'll have to do is wait at the foaling barn for night watch to get here.*

After she had checked the Maiden Barn and found all the horses accounted for safely, she followed the main road that would bring her towards the rest of the farm. The nearly hidden left hand turn leading to the back entrance of the farm caught her eye and she slammed on the brakes.

Bottles and cans were strewn along the edge of the side road. "Now I'll have to go get trash bags and clean this up," she moaned, resting her head on the steering wheel. She sat up, her fingers tapping on the steering wheel. *Why would there be trash along the side road no one uses?*

Furrowing her eyebrows, she cranked the wheel to the left and pulled onto the bumpy gravel drive. She wound through the heavily wooded path until she reached the clearing before the back gate. Looking over towards the ruins of the old assistant's cottage, she pulled over and parked the truck.

As she approached, she noted the rubble looked disturbed, fresh patches of dirt visible next to overturned concrete blocks. Millie experimentally held out her foot, measuring it against the boot print in the soil. It was larger than hers, but not by much, and judging from the impressions the tread had left behind, it was a pair of workbooks not unlike her own.

Millie crossed her arms as the breeze brought in a gust of cold air. Turning to head back to the truck, she looked back once more, finally noticing a polished white headstone. As she drew closer, her stomach flipped over.

Millie Wright
2005—2023

Chapter 20

M illie furrowed her eyebrows and had a strange feeling as she rounded the bend to the Yearling Barn. There was a silver Toyota parked behind the barn, beneath a row of pine trees. *Did Stewart forget to tell me that someone was coming?* But wouldn't they be parked in front of the barn in a parking spot? She pulled her cell phone from her back pocket and called Stewart.

The phone rang and rang, but all she got was his answering machine.

She was going to go find out what the silver car was about. Surely, it was just a mistake, someone showing up at the wrong time. Pulling up onto the green, she ignored the small signs cheerfully reminding passersby to please stay on the pavement.

Millie saw no one in the driver's seat of the car as the truck bumped along the uneven ground. She pulled even with the silver car and hopped out, taking care to not slam the door. Millie looked all around her and stood silently, listening for any sound. With the air quiet, she crept around to the side of the car, framing her hands against the glass to see inside. An Oaklyn sales catalog thrown on the passenger seat, a pair of leather loafers and a soda can were all Millie could see.

She hesitantly tested the door, disappointed to find it locked. Millie frowned and walked to the barn, her phone buzzing in her pocket. "Hello?"

"Millie, it's Stewart. I saw you called?"

"Yes," she replied, her voice soft as she crept inside. "Were we expecting anyone on the farm this evening?"

"No, not that I'm aware of..." Stewart trailed off. "Why, is there someone there?"

Millie hesitated. "I'm actually not sure. There's a car I don't recognize, parked behind the Yearling Barn. I haven't seen anyone though."

"Maybe someone got lost somehow," Stewart replied, sounding skeptical. "Do me a favor, and just look around for a few minutes. Let me know if you find anything out."

Millie ended the call and glanced down both sides of the barn aisle. It was cool and dark, quiet except for the chirping of birds in the rafters. All the horses were turned out for the night, giving the barn a hollow feel. She strode down the aisle, her boots echoing on the concrete.

"Hello?" she called out, first tentatively, then louder. Only the birds replied as she strode forward with determination.

Quick footsteps sounded from around the corner. Instinct took over, and Millie ducked into the nearest empty stall, crouched underneath the feed bucket. Her heart pounded in her chest so loudly she wondered if it could be heard. Millie's cell phone rang, shrilly breaking through the silence. Her stomach dropped as she desperately attempted to silence the phone.

With the ringer turned off, there was a long silence. Millie held her breath, hoping for the moment to pass.

"Hello?" called out a male voice. "Is anyone here?"

Footfalls crept along slowly, approaching Millie's stall. *Maybe,* she thought to herself, *if I play dumb, whoever this is will give me no trouble.* Her mouth was dry and her pulse raced as she stood up in the stall. Feeling eyes on her, she spun around to face a man.

"Mr. McConnell," Millie sputtered out, noting how strained her voice sounded. "I was just out here looking for my cell phone. I must have dropped it on my last round."

"Millie!" he exclaimed. His voice sounded entirely too loud for the stillness of the barn aisle. "What a nice surprise. Lovely night for a walk, eh?"

Millie blinked at him, guarded but kept her voice light. "Actually, I'm working the 4–7 shift. What are you up to?"

Riley's eyes darted back and forth. "I was just taking a look around. I spent a lot of time here as a child, just reminiscing is all." He let out a long sigh. "The past is in the past though, I suppose. I better be going now."

The hairs on the back of Millie's neck stood as Riley turned to leave. "How did you get the gate code, Riley?"

He turned back with a tight smile. "I just happened to be driving by as the feed truck was pulling in, I followed them. The Jennings' don't mind, they've invited me here before."

Millie nodded her head in understanding. "That's interesting, because feed and straw were delivered yesterday."

Riley held her gaze for a long moment, the corners of his mouth falling. "You're a bit of a spitfire, aren't you Millie? Come with me. I have something to show you." He roughly grabbed her arm and strode down the aisle, Millie stumbling to keep up.

Millie was frightened but fought the urge to resist. She knew she was no match in a fight, she would have to surprise him to get away.

Together they bee lined toward the feed room, Millie's mouth drying as she realized he intended to lock her in. Immediately before the door, Millie planted her feet and attempted to slip out of his grasp. Riley grabbed her shoulder and spun her around as she kicked him in the groin. Grunting in pain, he shoved Millie backwards through the door. Millie fell on her back, pain radiating through her skull. Before she could jump to her feet, the door had been slammed, though she could hear someone outside tinkering with the knob.

Millie lay still until the sound of footsteps had pounded away. She let out a shaky breath, flexing her fingers and toes, wincing as she sat up. The room was dark, a small window providing just enough illumination to see the outline of a wheelbarrow and feed bags. Millie rubbed at her blurry eyes, willing them to adjust to the darkness before unsteadily standing.

She wasn't surprised, but was disappointed when the feed door wouldn't budge after she tried shoving herself against it with all her might. With dismay, she noted that her phone screen was cracked and glitching. Millie was stuck, with only the mice to keep her company.

Hands on her hips, Millie assessed the situation. Locked door, no phone, no lights, stuck in an empty barn. Surely someone would find her by morning, or Connie would wonder why the truck was missing. But that all was hours away, Riley could be in another state by then.

Sighing, she sat down on the feed bags stacked neatly in the corner, the rich scent of sweet feed the only comfort in the room. She pressed her palms into her head, rubbing at her temples. What was Riley doing right now? Burning the manager's house to the ground? Separating foals from their mothers? Trying to injure innocent yearlings?

Millie slid off the grain bags and paced back and forth, her nerves crawling and curdling in her belly. *I have to do something,* she told herself. *I'm of no use just sitting here.*

Scanning the room thoughtfully, her eyes landed on the large wooden feed bin in the corner. Millie tested her weight against it. It was heavy, but when she pushed it, it wiggled on the concrete floor. *Could I move that under the window and stand on it?*

Millie took a deep breath and shoved her weight into the old wooden feed bin. Like fingernails on a chalkboard, the bins legs scraped at the floor, pushing old kernels of grain aside. Again, she shoved, wiggling it from side to side with all her might. It only moved a few inches at a time, but she made steady progress. Sweating and cursing under her breath from the exertion, Millie wiped her brow. *Not even halfway there,* she noted with irritation.

She glanced back where she had started, wrinkling her nose at the moldy bits of feed and a seemingly mummified mouse carcass that had resided underneath the bin. Her eyes drifted up to the walls—*is that an outline in the paneling?*

Millie's hands felt along the wall, tracing the subtle indent in the wood. She felt a thrill when the wood wiggled as she pressed into it, though her fingers couldn't grasp the edge to pull it out. Frustrated, she looked around for any possible tool to dislodge the panel, her gaze settling on the metal feed scoop. Determinedly, she jammed the edge of the scoop into the crack, pushing sideways in an attempt to wedge it out. With a pop, the panel broke loose and Millie pulled it away.

She reached her arm through the crawlspace sized hole in the wall. A wooden staircase leading down, but to what? With a pit in her stomach, Millie crawled through the hole and carefully made her descent.

A few steps down after feeling her way through some cobwebs, a thin string hung from a light bulb. Millie looked at it skeptically. *What are the odds of this working?*

With a gentle tug, the landing below was bathed in a yellow light. A few more steps, and she looked around, her breath catching in her throat. A large wooden desk pressed against the wall, with horse racing pictures hung from the stone walls.

Millie brushed dust away from the nearest picture, a galloping dark horse with its nose stretched over the finish line. She squinted at the faded lettering. **Round Top, Fayette Stakes Winner 1968**. Below it, a winners circle image. **Trieste, Del Mar Distaff 1971**. The mare stood proudly, her head raised and nostrils flaring. At her head was a tall man in a suit holding a young boy's hand. **Riley's first time at the races**, etched into a plate on the frame.

Millie approached the desk, eyeing the impressive collection of stallion halters hung on the wall like ducks in a row. She wasn't especially knowledgeable with Thoroughbred history, but even she recognized the impressive names written in the tarnished brass.

In the first drawer she opened, a cream colored envelope sat on top. *Riley* was scrawled across the back.

Momentarily, she considered that it was in bad form to read others mail, before deciding that social etiquette was voided the moment Riley locked her in a feed room. She opened the envelope with care, grasping at the delicate paper within, and unfolded the yellowed parchment.

Riley,

If you're reading this, I guess you finally found your way down into my thinking space, as I like to think of it. I suppose I'm gone by now, but just know I always hoped you would find your way here.

I'm assuming you're not thrilled with the way things turned out. How could you? The farm, the mares, all being sold off in the name of charity.

I've come to understand some things in my lifetime as a horseman. First, that the horse needs to come first, every single time. Without the horse, there is no sport, no reason for any of this.

Second, every person should have the opportunity to go out and find their own success. Only from the trials of creating a life you are proud of, can you learn the deep respect for the horses, land, and community we are surrounded by.

I look at you, so young and so full of potential. It's all out there for you, it really is. So I hope when you find this, in the place I told you it would be, that you will understand. I am sorry if you are disappointed with how things have turned out, and if you need to be angry with me, that's okay too.

Someday, you will have your own mares, your own farm, but first you need to struggle for it. I hope I've given you the tools you need to not just float, but swim.

All my love,
Uncle John

Millie pulled out the second piece of folded paper. Smoothing her thumb over the creases, her eyes scanned the top of the page. *The last will and testament of John McConnell.* The text went on to list John's assets, the farm, and dozens of mares. *To be sold at public auction, with the proceeds to be donated to Birch Haven Thoroughbred Retirement Center and North American*

173

Jockey's Distress Fund.

After one last cursory look around, she set down the will and cracked open the door at the far side of the room. Through the door, the air was cooler and musty smelling. Despite the darkness, Millie recognized the same sort of tunnel that previously had led her to the Jennings' house. Feeling along the wall, she found a small light switch, illuminating the tunnel in a dull light. "Until next time," she spoke to the room, before striding out into the tunnel.

Millie went as fast as she could, half walking, half jogging, though she found it difficult to run while she was hyperventilating. The tunnel twisted and turned in front of her, giving away no secrets. *One more step, one more breath,* she muttered to herself over and over. The stone dust floor crunched beneath her, the cold walls echoing her footfalls back at her.

A small staircase appeared, smaller than the one that led to the manager's house. At the top was an old door. Before opening it, Millie pressed her ear to the crack. Hearing nothing, she carefully turned the knob, cringing as the hinges sang their disapproval.

Braced for anything, she swung the door open. Looking up, she blinked in confusion. Covering the doorway was a large sheet of plywood, though a thin line of light at the bottom of the door promised that *something* was on the other side. Millie leaned her weight into the panel, pushing and kneeing it with all her strength. Though it flexed, the nails didn't budge.

I need a hammer, or at least something blunt to slam into this. Glancing around the room, she searched for anything that might help. The lantern waiting patiently by the blocked door was too delicate. Millie doubted that the lone brick on the ground would be of much assistance. Glancing behind the staircase, there was one object of interest, a curved metal crowbar. She grabbed it, surprised at the weight.

She carried it up to the doorway, throwing her weight into the board to make a gap big enough to shove the bar into. Once it was wedged in, she took a deep breath and began pulling. A thrill ran through her when she felt it working. She could feel the weakness of the nails, how they were slipping right out of the soft wood.

With a sudden pop, the plywood came undone on the right side, providing a gap just big enough for Millie to slip through. With a backward glance at the tunnel, she slithered through sideways.

Chapter 21

Sighing in relief, Millie looked around. She was in the maintenance building. The doors were closed, the lights off, but at least she knew where she was. Glancing back at the opening, she realized she had been behind the wall map of the farm. *Guess that extra room off the Yearling Barn wasn't a mistake on the map after all,* she snickered.

She strode towards the office, her heart pounding. There was a phone in there, but who to call? The police? Stewart? She grabbed the door handle, cursing between gritted teeth when it wouldn't turn. Locked. Crouching down, she grabbed a hairpin out of her bun and jammed it in the lock, massaging it until she heard the telltale click.

A brief internal debate ensued, and Millie chose to call Stewart first. *Is locking someone in a room actually a crime?* She wondered to herself. Anyways, they would take ages to get to the rural farm, and she couldn't afford to waste any time.

Shifting her weight and drumming her fingers, she waited. One ring, two rings, no answer. She slammed the phone back on the hook huffed in exasperation. Next to the phone, scribbled on yellowed notepaper was a list of contacts Plumbing, heating, excavation numbers, and... Joe!

176

He sounded confused when he answered the phone. "Hello?" "Joe," she rushed out. "I need your help, it would take too long to explain everything. I need to know how to look at the security cameras and lock the gates. It's an emergency."

"Millie? What are you talking about, are you okay? Why are you calling from the farm maintenance line?"

"It's fine, I'm fine, but I need to know. Like, right now."

"Alright, but I'm calling the police after we hang up."

Millie began to protest. Joe cut her off. "First you need to get into the office. The keys are underneath the doormat outside of it."

"I broke into the office," she rushed out, exasperated. "That's where I'm calling from."

Joe paused. "Now that I think of it, that seems kind of obvious, sorry." He cleared his throat, "In the corner there's a small TV, you see it? There's a remote on top of it, you need to turn it on. It should show security footage. You can change cameras by changing the channel."

Millie clicked through the channels desperately. Had he gotten away?

Joe's voice cut through her frazzled chain of thought. "To lock the gates, there is a switch on the wall behind the desk. When you pull it down, it will lock the farm gates, unless you have an override code for the keypad. That's just so emergency vehicles can still get in.

"But Millie," Joe warned, "locking the gates won't stop someone from climbing the perimeter fence to leave. All it means is no one can get in or out of the farm by car."

"Okay," she replied with grim determination. Thinking of Riley's stout figure and stiff gait, she struggled to imagine him climbing the tall fence and hedges. "I have to run now. But thank you Joe, truly. You've been an enormous help."

"It's no problem Millie. I'm calling the police now. Just," he paused. "please... be careful."

After hanging up, she returned to the television, flipping through the cameras, her breath catching. Riley's car was parked crookedly behind a line of rose bushes near the Jennings' house. Millie knew she had to confront him before he did something rash. She mentally calculated how long it would take to run. *Too long,* she told herself. Walking out of the office, she found herself looking up at the farm's commercial sized tractor they used for mowing. *I guess this will have to do.*

It took Millie a few moments to figure out how to raise the garage doors so she could actually get out, then she had to situate herself inside the tractor. Aside from its massive size and ensuing struggle to back it out of the garage safely, Millie found it relatively straightforward to drive.

She wasn't sure why it had been in the shop in the first place, and she hoped whatever was wrong with it wouldn't affect its speed. The gears ground a bit when she shifted it into a higher gear, but it was still chugging along at a steady twenty miles per hour towards the manager's house.

When Millie was about a mile away, she realized that her vehicle of choice was going to give away her arrival if she drove right up to the house. She pulled over and stopped, carefully climbing down the steps. The sky was darkening, the air biting at her bare arms.

She jogged towards the house, her footfalls gently thudding on the grass, slowing as she drew closer. It seemed too obvious to enter through the front door, so she crept around to the back of the house.

She hoped to enter through the back porch, but she wasn't

sure where Riley was in the house. She found herself attempting to peek through the windows as she walked, tripping over the shrubbery. Seeing no signs of him, she opened a screen door to the porch, wincing as the door spring creaked.

Her heart jumped when a wind gust blew a wind chime, but continued on towards the door. Crouching down below the back door, she slowly raised herself until she could just see into the mud room. It appeared still and silent, so she walked through the door.

Inside she moved towards the kitchen, then stood unmoving. What *was* her plan? Riley had already proven he was willing to hurt her when he shoved her into the feed room. Maybe she should have waited for the police. *It's too late now.*

A short curtain rod was propped up by the door. She grabbed it as an afterthought, feeling ridiculous as she clutched the flimsy fiberglass.

At the sound of hurried footsteps, Millie's breath caught in her throat. "It's *got* to be in here somewhere," a low male voice muttered.

A loud crash disrupted the stillness of the house. Millie's hands shook as she looked into the next room. Riley stared into a hole in the wall, a hatchet propped against the wall next to him. "Where did you put it, old man?!" Riley spit out, before picking up the hatchet to focus on another section of wall.

Millie knew she was quick, but she didn't feel confident that her little curtain rod would be any match for Riley's hatchet, if it came to that. She stepped backwards with care, wishing to remain unnoticed. She was so close to the back door, to being able to bolt to safety and wait for the police. But then she stepped on the world's creakiest floorboard.

"Who's there?" shouted Riley, his voice drawing closer.

Millie froze, and judged her distance to the door. If she moved quickly, she might be able to dash out before Riley could stop her. Diving for the doorknob, she twisted it free, until she was slammed into the floor. Her elbow screamed in pain, but Millie felt as though she was in a haze as Riley glared down at her. "Girl, has nobody ever told you to mind your own business? Because I'm telling you, right now."

Though the ceiling lights made it hard to focus, Millie blinked up at him. "To be fair sir, you kind of involved me in your business when you shoved me into the feed room."

He sighed. "And if you had just stayed in there, *like you were supposed to*, someone would have eventually come by and freed you."

Millie shrugged. She felt very casual, despite her current position. When she began talking, her voice sounded far away. "I think the police are on the way."

"Now why would you have done something like that, Millie? There was no need to call the police. My little treasure hunt isn't hurting anyone."

"Well, except for the Jennings'. It isn't great for them, how you've been sabotaging the farm."

Riley rolled his eyes. "I would hardly call it sabotage. More like, helping them see that this farm is too much for them. There's no shame in it really, they just bit off more than they could chew. Too inexperienced to run a farm of this prestige, plus, it's just not in their blood."

Millie nodded. "Yes, that's how your uncle said he felt in his letter. Too much, too soon is a bad recipe for anyone wanting to make their own way in this world."

"Letter?" Riley barked. "What letter?!"

She shrugged, noncommittally. "I found it in a hidden room

off the Yearling Barn. I think it was addressed to you."

Riley's eyes were wide and erratic. He lowered his hatchet to poke Millie's back. "Take me there. I want to see this hidden room, right now."

Millie stood unsteadily. "Sure, it's a bit of a walk though."

"We'll drive," He snapped.

Riley kept the hatchet pressed up against her back the entire walk to the car. Wordlessly, they climbed in the car and he drove to the Yearling Barn. *Where are the police?* Millie wondered. It was a large farm of several hundred acres, easy to get lost within, but they weren't exactly hidden, driving Riley's old Toyota through the center of the main road.

When they arrived, Riley pulled behind the barn so the car was hidden. He looked over at her with contempt. "Show me the way. But just know I still have this with me," raising his hatchet.

Millie's stomach churned as she did as she was told. She was getting more concerned with her predicament by the moment, but was sure there was an escape opportunity somewhere—if only she was clever enough to see it.

Riley scoffed behind her as she opened the door to the feed room. "You think I'm stupid enough to fall for this? You're not going to trap me in here, if that's what you're thinking."

Millie shook her head. "Follow me, and you'll see for yourself," she said in a level tone. "I only found it because I had some time to kill in here earlier. Had to keep myself entertained."

Riley furrowed his eyebrows and followed without speaking. As he grunted and struggled to wriggle through the crawlspace entrance, Millie fleetingly hoped that he would get stuck, not looking back as she descended the staircase.

She tugged the lights on, disappointed to hear Riley walking down the steps, his breath catching as he caught sight of the room. "You weren't kidding," he muttered in amazement, staring up at the photos lining the walls. His fingers brushed the dust away from the winners circle photo. "I remember this."

Millie stood with uncertainty, watching on as Riley studied every photo. The trance was broken with an abrupt *Meow*. Millie looked up the stairs, confused. The calico cat from the tree in the field, stood at the top, unblinking. "Is the calico cat yours?" she asked Riley.

"Mine? No, I wouldn't say so. My family used to breed calico cats, I imagine she must be the last of the line. I bring her food sometimes, only because clearly no one else cares," he spit out with a sneer.

Millie looked up again, the calico cat still staring with intense green eyes. The cat dropped her chin, as if to nod. Millie glanced back behind her, Riley hunched over the wooden desk. The cat squeaked out another *meow*, before trotting through the crawlspace, looking back at Millie the whole time.

This is it, she told herself. She stepped back gently, Riley too enamored with the contents of the letter to notice. At the bottom of the staircase, she took a deep breath, and sprinted to the top.

"Hey. Hey! Where do you think you're going!" Riley screamed behind her. *Don't look back, don't look back.*

In one quick movement, she dropped down and threw herself through the crawlspace, jumping up on the other side to sprint to the feed room door. She could hear Riley's yells, feel his anger, but she was too far ahead for it to matter. She slammed and locked the feed room door, her frenzied brain thinking of nothing except getting to the maintenance building to lock the other door.

The farm night watch truck was still parked behind the Yearling Barn, where Millie had left it earlier. She yanked on the door handle, scrambling inside to turn on the engine. The sky had grown dark, Millie had to turn on the headlights to see the paved drive ahead. She drove as fast as she dared, wincing as the old truck made strange noises the faster she went.

It was a short drive. Millie braked hard, the tires squealing as she threw the truck in park. Bolting to the map on the wall, she threw herself against the wall to close the gap. Her eyes searched desperately for something, anything, to prop against it.

A heavy wooden desk sat in the corner. Millie wasn't sure she would be able to move it but she had to try. Inch by inch she dragged it, making a frustratingly small amount of progress. She wondered how long it would take Riley to find the end of the tunnel, and felt another surge of adrenaline.

"Millie!" a sharp voice called out. "Are you in here?"

"Joe?" she cried out. "I'm by the map on the wall, I need your help!"

Hurried footsteps rounded the corner. Joe looked alarmed. "What is going on? Are you okay?" he asked, his voice urgent.

Millie shook her head. "I'll explain in a minute, but we need to move this desk *now*."

With Joe pushing, the desk moved easier, and they got it wedged against the wall. Sirens sounded distantly.

Millie leaned back into the wall, and slid down to the floor as the gravity of the past few hours hit her. She felt herself crumble, burying her face in her hands.

Joe crouched down next to her, placing a tentative hand on her back. "Hey," he whispered, his eyes locking onto hers. "It's okay. You're okay now."

The sirens sounded as if they were directly outside the

maintenance building now. Millie wiped her eyes and stood up. Joe looked at her with concern. She gave him a thin smile. "Later. I have to go tell the police what's going on." She paused for a moment. "And Joe... Thank you."

Joe nodded. "You know where to find me."

Chapter 22

Millie felt like she was living in a strange sort of dream the rest of the evening, her body floating along through the motions. There was the stress of Riley being arrested, then dealing with police questioning, while still trying to watch the mares on video cameras until Connie arrived for her night shift.

In the midst of all of this, Richard and Kelly Jennings returned from the hospital in Louisville, dismayed at the excitement they found upon their arrival. Richard was in a wheelchair, but assured her he would be back on his feet soon enough.

Joe stayed with Millie, following her at a distance. He didn't say much, but she appreciated his presence, steady and quiet.

It was almost dark now. She had sent Joe home, reassuring him that she was okay. She wasn't *actually* sure she was okay, but she felt like she had to be alone, and so she crept around the farm like a cat in the dark. The crickets chirped and her feet led her to a pasture fence where some of the younger maiden mares stood. A chocolate colored mare, Moccasin, pushed her way to the front, her ears flicking back to warn away her friends. She pushed her soft muzzle into Millie's palms and blinked at her inquisitively. *Do you have any cookies for me?*

Millie smiled, pushing her away as the mare nipped gently at her hands. She kept walking, her eyes landing on the Jennings' house, lit from within and somehow looking larger and more imposing now that it was occupied. *As it should be.*

She rounded a bend in the drive, and froze instantly. A male figure strolled through the small graveyard. Her pulse quickened, she wanted to run but was terrified of drawing attention to herself. *Maybe if I just slowly back up...*

"Millie?" A deep voice called out. "Is that you?"

Millie let out a deep breath of relief, her gut still twisting with nerves. When she spoke, her voice shook. "It's me."

Stewart stood inside the graveyard, with large tan gardening gloves pulled up his forearms, hands on a shovel. "We really must stop meeting this way!" he declared, his voice chipper.

Millie eyed him suspiciously. "You realize I'm going to have to ask what you are doing? Why does it look like you're digging up graves?"

Stewart winced, glancing down at himself. "I supposed I didn't consider how this would look. If it makes you feel better though, I was planting flowers, not exhuming bodies. Would you like to see?"

Millie peeked over the stone wall, the pink and white flowers popping against the navy sky. "Tell me Stewart, do you do all of your digging after dark?"

Stewart rubbed the back of his neck uncomfortably. "Frankly I was too worked up after this evening to just go home like it was business as usual. And to be honest, I haven't been entirely truthful with you."

Millie snorted in disdain, Stewart clearing his throat and ignoring her. "I like to keep the graves here tidy because they are my family. Very distantly," he added hurriedly.

Millie blinked in amazement. "You're related to the Mc-Connell's?"

"No, no," he shook his head. "Even further back than that, the people that Joseph McConnell originally bought the land from almost one hundred years ago. I had no idea when I started working here. I got onto a genealogy kick after my grandfather passed away, and realized that some of the names in my family tree were names in this very graveyard. From there, I started asking around my extended family. Almost nobody knew what I was talking about, but my grandmother said *her* grandfather told her stories about the farm and what a whimsical place it was. She said he was always leaving valuable things in strange places here, digging up gold coins, that sort of thing."

"So you thought you would take a look for yourself?" Millie asked.

To Stewart's credit, he at least had the grace to look ashamed. "I know it's wrong. I swear I hardly ever search. It was just with the weird things going on, I had wondered if that had anything to do with it."

Millie shrugged. "I probably would have had the same thought."

Stewart frowned. "I'm really sorry about sticking you with that shift. And being a difficult manager in general. Good news is, the professionals are back, so I can go back to running my Yearling Barn in peace."

Millie smiled. "You were doing the best you could under a lot of stress. And if I hadn't been working tonight, who knows if Riley would have been caught red handed."

"So we're good?" he asked, his voice hopeful.

"We're all good," Millie confirmed. "I'm going to continue my walk. Happy digging," she called over her shoulder, laughing.

Ducking down a side path that would lead her past the yearling filly field, she heard a pitiful mew. Squinting through the fading light, her eyes landed on the tiny calico cat who had led her to the tunnels, and ultimately assisted in her escape. "You," she declared, "Are a very special cat. Did you know that?"

The calico blinked at her, flicking her tail as if to say *Duh*. She carefully stepped forward to meet Millie, twirling around her ankles.

"You're going to trip me," Millie giggled, reaching a hand down. The cat flinched, then relaxed into her touch. Scratching the cat's back, Millie had a troubling thought. "Who is going to take care of you now that Riley won't be bringing food to that tree?"

Large green eyes stared back at Millie. *You will.*

She crouched down and picked up the cat, burying her face in her soft fur. Millie had known it was a small cat, but was shocked at how tiny her frame was underneath her fluff. "You can't weight more than five or six pounds, sweetie," she cooed. The cat squinted her eyes and purred, melting into Millie's touch as she scratched her chin.

"What would you think," she began deep in thought, "Of being my cat? I can offer you food, water, and a bed to sleep on. All I ask in exchange is that you keep my feet warm when winter comes. Deal?"

The cat purred deeply, like a tiny locomotive against Millie's chest. *Deal.*

Dear Dad,

I saw on the forecast that Maine is getting some pretty crazy storms, I hope you're doing okay.

I'm going to leave Willowmere, just as soon as I can work up the nerve to give Mr. Jennings my notice. It feels odd to give a two week notice when I've barely been here a week, but if I didn't, I think I would feel even worse than I already do.

Willowmere is gorgeous and mysterious. Since I've been here, I've learned more about its history and prior occupants than I ever imagined I would (or frankly wanted!). Home to a graveyard, underground tunnels, some very moody electronics, and even moodier mares and foals, it does not lack character in the least.

I don't want you to worry, but I want to be honest. The reason I'm leaving is because of some weird things that happened here. Ghost sightings, threatening notes, planted wasps nests, loose horses, and suspicious power outages were all just another day on the farm.

Long story short, Riley McConnell was the last remaining blood relative of the McConnell family, who built this farm. Left empty handed when his uncle passed away unexpectedly many years ago, he recently ran into financial troubles.

Today, thanks to police questioning, Riley admitted his grand plan was to scare everyone off by sabotaging the farm so he could properly search for his uncle's alleged secret treasure. Once he sold it, he was going to buy out the Jennings' for cheap, and all would be right in the world. Or something like that.

I think it's all been resolved now, at least I hope. Riley is in police custody, and Richard and Kelly are back to running their farm as usual. I can't help but have the feeling I need to move on though. When I began to really think about it, I wondered if I would ever truly feel safe around here. Would lights flickering ever just be a faulty light bulb? A loose horse a silly mistake? I don't know if I'll ever be able to let go of the things I've seen and heard here. I'm struggling a bit to figure out if that's okay.

On the bright side, I foaled out my very first mare here and learned lots about horse husbandry. I loved being on the farm and around the horses, enough that I put a few calls out to see what else is available in Kentucky.

I think Mom wants me back in Vermont for the summer after hearing about all this drama, but I just got an email back from an FEI ranked endurance rider who wants to talk to me tomorrow. She needs a summer working student to help condition her mounts, and help host an endurance ride about an hour from here. It sounds like a blast—keep your fingers crossed for me!

Happy trails, and please call me when you can.

Love,

Millie

About the Author

Hailing from the Vermont/New Hampshire border, Avery Taylor has been around horses her entire life. She has held a wide variety of jobs in the equine industry, from veterinary assistant, to exercise rider, camp counselor, and caring for mares and their newborn foals.

She currently resides in Central Kentucky with five horses, four cats, and two dogs. When she's not writing, you can usually find her riding or hiking in one of the Bluegrass regions' many beautiful parks. *Whispers at Willowmere Farm* is her first book.

Made in the USA
Las Vegas, NV
17 December 2024